"What are you doing out here?"

Eli stuck his head inside. "I came to check on you. You all right?"

She studied him by the light of a kerosene lantern someone had hung on a pole outside the barn door. "I'm fine." She looked down at her hands in her lap and sniffed. "Why wouldn't I be?"

He glanced up into the sky, the broad brim of his wool hat casting a shadow across his face. "Starting to rain." He hesitated. "Would it be all right if I came inside with you?"

Though Ginger's head was down, she could feel his gaze on her. "Sure," she said. She didn't know that she wanted any company right now, but if she was going to choose someone to be there, it would be Eli.

She moved over to the driver's side. This buggy had a split front seat, which allowed one to easily get to the rear benches that faced each other.

Eli got inside and closed the door. And suddenly the buggy seemed smaller.

And more intimate.

Emma Miller lives quietly in her old farmhouse in rural Delaware. Fortunate enough to have been born into a family of strong faith, she grew up on a dairy farm, surrounded by loving parents, siblings, grandparents, aunts, uncles and cousins. Emma was educated in local schools and once taught in an Amish schoolhouse. When she's not caring for her large family, reading and writing are her favorite pastimes.

Books by Emma Miller

Love Inspired

The Amish Spinster's Courtship
The Christmas Courtship
A Summer Amish Courtship
An Amish Holiday Courtship

The Amish Matchmaker

A Match for Addy
A Husband for Mari
A Beau for Katie
A Love for Leah
A Groom for Ruby
A Man for Honor

Visit the Author Profile page
at Harlequin.com for more titles.

An Amish Holiday Courtship

Emma Miller

LOVE INSPIRED
INSPIRATIONAL ROMANCE

PIF
Miller

LOVE INSPIRED®

INSPIRATIONAL ROMANCE

Recycling programs
for this product may
not exist in your area.

ISBN-13: 978-1-335-48853-4

An Amish Holiday Courtship

Copyright © 2020 by Emma Miller

This edition published by arrangement with Harlequin Books S.A.

For questions and comments about the quality of this book,
please contact us at CustomerService@Harlequin.com.

Love Inspired
22 Adelaide St. West, 40th Floor
Toronto, Ontario M5H 4E3, Canada
www.Harlequin.com

Printed in U.S.A.

Can two walk together, except they be agreed?
—*Amos* 3:3

Chapter One

Ginger Stutzman followed her mother down the baking aisle of Byler's store pushing a grocery cart. They'd come midday because her sister wanted to make *rosina kuchen*. Tara made the best raisin pie in Kent County, hands down. She'd been halfway through the recipe when she realized she was short a full cup of raisins, and their mother had offered to run to Byler's as she already had a list of items to pick up. Ginger had volunteered to accompany their mother because she genuinely enjoyed grocery shopping, but also because she knew the young man she was sweet on, Joe Verkler, frequented Byler's at that time of day. Not only did the store sell groceries and kitchen goods, and even woodstoves, but they also had a deli where sandwiches were made. Amish work crews often stopped there for lunch, and Joe had mentioned after church the previous Sunday that he was overseeing a work crew nearby. She hoped that she might *accidentally* bump into him.

"Let's see, dark brown sugar and white whole wheat flour," Ginger's mother, Rosemary, read off a list from the back of an envelope. "Anything else you can think of that we need baking-wise?" She glanced up, her new reading glasses perched on the end of her nose. She'd resisted buying the eyeglasses, hating to admit that she was at an age that she needed them, but she was finding they made her life easier.

"*Ne*, nothing that I can think of," Ginger replied, searching for Joe, but trying hard not to appear to be looking for anyone. To her delight, as she reached the end of the aisle, sure enough, she spotted him.

Joe Verkler was standing near the deli counter, waiting to place an order, a white numbered ticket in his hand. She smiled the moment she saw him and was pleased that she was wearing her favorite dress, a rose-colored one that he'd remarked on the first time they met. It had been three weeks ago, at a barn raising in nearby Seven Poplars. Joe had only just arrived from Lancaster County, Pennsylvania, and had struck up a bold conversation with her, saying he was new in town and wanted to get to know all the pretty, single girls.

Joe was what Ginger's mother called *a man too handsome for his own good*. He was tall and broad shouldered, with golden hair that tumbled almost to his shoulders and a dimple on his square chin. He was clean-shaven, of course, meaning he was unmarried. And though he wore the typical Amish male clothing of homemade denim trousers and a colored shirt under his denim coat, his suspenders were a fancy braided leather. Today he was sporting a pair of black Nike running shoes. It was something not seen among the Amish in Kent County and a bit of scandal, according to her friend Martha Gruber's mother, Eunice. Apparently, all of the mothers in Hickory Grove were in a tizzy over Joe's flashy looks and his choice of footwear. Most Amish men wore sturdy work boots or rubber boots if the weather was poor. No one wore name-brand items for fear of appearing too much like an Englisher. But the Amish church districts of Lancaster County were less strict than locally; that's what Martha said. Martha was practically engaged to be married to a boy from Lancaster, so if anyone knew such things, she would.

"Oh dear, the raisins!" Ginger's mother chuckled. "We can't forget the raisins, can we? Now where did they get to? The next aisle, maybe?" she asked, walking past Ginger.

Ginger waited for her mother to go down the next aisle and then eased the cart that was already half-full off to the side so other shoppers could get by. Even a midweek grocery run for their family was a full cart. It took a lot of food to feed the sixteen adults and children who ate at her mother and stepfather's two kitchen tables. Pinching her cheeks to give them color, Ginger pretended to be interested in a display of iced gingerbread cookies at the endcap. She took a quick peek in Joe's direction, and then when he turned his head, she quickly reached for one.

"Ginger!" Joe called.

When she didn't answer right away, she saw him, out of the corner of her eye, walk toward her. "Ginger Stutzman?"

She turned to him, pretending to be surprised. Then she smiled her prettiest smile. "Joe."

"I thought that was you," he exclaimed, hooking his thumbs beneath his suspenders.

"What a surprise, seeing you here." She returned the cookies to the shelf. They didn't buy packaged sweets, not when Tara was such a good baker.

"I'm ordering a sandwich." He pointed in the direction of the deli counter. "Waiting my turn."

One of the clerks called out the next number and a tall, thin English woman carrying a baby on her back hurried toward the counter. "Do you have smoked turkey?" she asked, seeming quite harried.

Ginger looked back at Joe. He had big, gorgeous hazel eyes. "What kind of sandwich?" she asked, tucking her hands behind her back.

He was grinning at her and she felt her cheeks flush. She knew that *hochmut* was something frowned upon by the Amish. Especially pride in one's looks. After all, that was just a matter of who your parents were, but Martha said that she and Joe made a fetching couple— him being so handsome and Ginger being the prettiest girl in the county.

At twenty-four, Ginger had been walking out with boys for years. She had been in no hurry to get serious, though, and had enjoyed the liberty given by her mother and stepfather to get to know as many young men as possible. She knew she was blessed that they had given her the freedom to figure out what kind of man she wanted to marry. She'd gone to church suppers and picnics and more singings than she could count. But now, with her twenty-fifth birthday approaching, she was beginning to think about settling down. Like every Amish girl, she dreamed of having a husband and children. And handsome Joe Verkler was just the kind of man she thought she ought to marry.

"I ordered a spicy Italian sub," Joe responded, holding her gaze. He wore a pair of sunglasses perched on his forehead, below his navy knit beanie. The glasses looked expensive, not like the ones her brothers bought at Spence's Bazaar, two pairs for ten dollars. "With lettuce, tomato and hot peppers," he added. "I love hot peppers."

"You didn't pack your lunch?" Ginger teased. "My *mam* says buying out can be expensive. My brothers pack when they work away from home."

He shrugged his broad shoulders. "I hate to trouble my aunt Edna. She and my uncle Ader have been kind enough to let me stay with them. She's got a houseful of little ones and enough work without me adding tasks to her morning." He made a face. "Besides, she makes terrible sandwiches. Too much mayonnaise."

It was on the tip of Ginger's tongue to suggest he could make his own sandwich for lunch, but she held back the comment. She didn't want to seem shrewish. Maybe men didn't make their own lunches in Lancaster. While the kitchen was certainly a woman's domain in her mother's house, her stepfather wasn't above making his own peanut butter and honey sandwich, and her stepbrothers all knew how to make their own coffee and sweep a floor.

"So… You here alone?" Joe asked. He was practically out-and-out flirting with her right there in the middle of the store for anyone to see.

The place was busy as always with English and

Amish alike. It was a good store to catch a bargain. And maybe a good place to catch a husband, Ginger thought.

"Alone? Of course not." Ginger smiled and rolled her eyes as if Joe had just said the silliest thing. "I'm here with my *mam.* My sister Tara is making *rosina kuchen* and we ran out of raisins."

"Too bad." Joe knitted his thick brows. "About you not being here alone. Not about the raisins. Because if you were here on your own, I'd offer you a ride home. I've got my rig here." He pointed in the direction of the side parking lot where folks could safely leave a horse and buggy. "A two-seater. Built it myself in two weeks. You know, after work and chores."

Ginger's stepfather had built several buggies in his shop, so she knew how much time went into such a project. It was hardly something one could build in a few weeks. A few months was more like it, but she just smiled up at him, nodding. If Joe wanted to impress her, who was she to correct him on such a small detail?

"*Atch*, there you are." Ginger's mother appeared from around the corner. "I found the raisins and lost you, *Dochtah*." A box of raisins in one hand and the list in the other, she took in Joe, measuring him up.

Ginger could tell right away by the purse of her mother's mouth that she didn't approve. "Um, you remember Joe Verkler," she introduced. "You met him at Rufus Yoder's barn raising? He's staying with his aunt and uncle, Ader and Edna Verkler. Joe's from Lancaster County," she added.

"Good to see you again, Rosemary." Joe fiddled with the numbered ticket he held in his hand.

"And you, Joe." Without a smile, her mother returned

her attention to the list on the envelope. "I forgot lettuce, Ginger. Could you fetch it? Three heads of romaine."

Just then, their neighbor Eli Kutz came walking their way carrying a handbasket. Ginger couldn't help but notice that it was filled with individual servings of pre-made pudding and Jell-O, as well as store-bought cookies and snack cakes. Two red packages of iced ginger cookies teetered on the top.

"Rosemary, Ginger," he exclaimed, his face lighting up with genuine pleasure.

Eli was a widower and older than Ginger, maybe in his midthirties. He wasn't an ugly man, but he wasn't what a girl would call handsome, either. Not like Joe. But she liked Eli, as did everyone in her family. He had been the first neighbor to extend his hand in friendship when they moved from New York to Delaware almost three years ago. His kindness had particularly touched Ginger. His wife had only recently passed, yet he had appeared at their door bearing honey from his own combs and a smile that was always on his face, despite his trials.

"Eli, have you met Joe Verkler?" Ginger went through the introductions again and then explained to Joe where Eli lived. Eli hadn't been at the barn raising, as his daughter was ill, and Joe didn't belong to their same church district, so she doubted the two men had crossed paths.

"Forty-nine!" the clerk at the deli counter called loudly, sounding annoyed. "Last time. Forty-nine!"

"That's me." Joe held up his ticket as if it were a prize. "Be right back."

Rosemary offered a quick smile, but her lips were

pressed tightly together as if it pained her. She rolled their cart closer and dropped in the raisins.

"I'll wait right here," Ginger told Joe, watching him as he hurried toward the deli counter. He was a fine-looking man, broad shouldered and tall.

"How is Lizzy?" Rosemary asked, giving Eli her full attention. "Eunice said Lizzy was due for a pediatrician's visit this morning." She didn't have to explain which Eunice she meant, though there were two in Hickory Grove. She meant Eunice Gruber, her friend Martha's mother. Eunice knew everything that went on in their little town, sometimes things that weren't meant to be known.

"She's doing better. Much better." Eli set the red plastic basket of goodies at his feet. "The doctor says she expects a full recovery, but Lizzy's still on bed rest. She's only to get up a few times a day yet, her being so weak."

"Our prayers were answered," Rosemary murmured. "I know you must be relieved she's recovering."

"We all are, my boys and, of course, my sister and her family." Eli looked to Ginger. "I haven't had a chance to thank you for the little doll you made for Lizzy that you sent with the chicken soup last week. Lizzy won't let it out of her sight."

"I'm glad she liked it," Ginger said. "And so glad she's going to be okay."

The little girl had suffered complications from the chicken pox and had been hospitalized two weeks previously for several days due to dehydration. Lizzy, almost four years old, was a sweet little girl, and Ginger felt so sorry for her. When she was sick as a child, she remembered how she had wanted no one but her *mam*.

She couldn't imagine what it was like to be motherless at such a young age.

"I'm thankful, indeed, for her improvement." Eli adjusted the wide-brimmed wool hat perched on his head. Unlike the younger men like Joe and her brothers, he wore more conservative attire to town. "I'm in a bit of a bind now, though, with Mary Yoder married and moving to Kentucky." He was referring to the twenty-one-year-old who used to babysit for him. With four little ones, Eli cared for his children most of the time on his own, but that meant grocery shopping and doing the laundry on top of barn and field work. Ginger couldn't imagine how he did it all without full-time help.

Joe joined the group again. "I got the big sub. A man my size needs a healthy-sized sandwich to keep up his strength. But they are out of hot peppers, and I'm sorely disappointed. I had a mind for hot peppers on my sandwich."

Rosemary stared at Joe, her face expressionless. Then she turned back to Eli. "You were saying you have a problem?"

Ginger rolled her eyes. What her mother was suggesting with that look was that Joe didn't know what real problems were. Thankfully, he didn't notice, didn't understand or didn't care.

"*Ya*, I'm not sure what to do." Eli pressed his hand to his forehead. "Ader Verkler—I'm guessing that's your uncle." Eli looked at Joe and then back to the women. "He hired me to build the wood paneling on a fireplace. His client wants it all handmade." He motioned with both hands. "Built-ins on two sides. All custom plans. It's a good eight to ten weeks of work. Put me right through to Christmas."

"Such beautiful work you do, Eli," Rosemary said. "Properly *Plain*, but still so beautiful. A talent like that is God-given."

"It doesn't even have to be *Plain*," Eli explained. "The clients are Englishers. Moved here from New Jersey and have their heart set on Amish builders. Anyway, trouble is, now with Mary gone, I've no one to watch the little ones while I go off to work. I can bring one or two of the bigger boys along at a time, but Lizzy's still in bed." He chuckled. "And to tell the truth, I'm afraid Phillip's not well behaved enough to set loose on a job site. I can't imagine what he might get into."

Ginger and her mother both smiled. Five-year-old Phillip wasn't a bad child, but he could be naughty. At a fundraiser supper recently, Phillip had been caught fishing cherries out of a dozen cherry pies meant to be served for dessert. And not long before that, he filled his aunt Claudia's rubber boots with milk fresh from the morning milking. To make matters worse, the milk had sat all day, curdled and made quite a stink not only to the mudroom but also to his aunt's stockings.

"I thought your sister was helping out," Ginger said, filled with concern for Eli and his family. She imagined the additional income was important. He farmed, of course, but like most Amish men in the community, he supplemented that income with outside work.

"*Ya*, she helps out. She was a blessing when Lizzy was at her sickest. But Claudia has a family of her own, her own house to attend to." He shook his head. "I hate to turn down the work. Like I said, it would only be until Christmas, but I'm at a loss as to what to do."

Ginger's mother glanced at Ginger. Her mother didn't have to say anything; Ginger knew what she was thinking and nodded.

Her mother looked back at Eli. "What would you think of Ginger lending a hand? She's good with children, and I know she'd be happy to help, wouldn't you?"

"*Ya,* I could watch Lizzy," Ginger said, excited by the prospect. "And the boys, too," she added, thinking it might be good for Eli to spend some time without his children rather than taking them to work with him. Every parent needed a break. She had learned that from her mother. "As long as *Mam* and Benjamin can spare me." She was old enough not to have to ask permission to do something, but because she had plenty of chores at home and also worked at her stepfather's harness shop, she wanted to be sure it wouldn't cause too much upset in the family. In order for her to work for Eli, others would have to do her jobs at home.

"Spare you?" Her mother chuckled. "I've got too many cooks in my kitchen as is. And I'm sure Benjamin can find someone to cover your shifts." She eyed Eli. "Always underfoot, my girls. I keep hoping they'll start marrying, but they don't seem in any great hurry."

"*Mam!*" Ginger laughed nervously. She stole a quick look in Joe's direction. He grinned.

Eli turned to Ginger, his blue eyes twinkling. "Would you consider watching my children? Lizzy adores you, you know. I think she'd heal all the quicker having you there at the house. And I'd pay you, of course," he added quickly.

Ginger pressed her lips together, touched that Eli thought she could assist in Lizzy's recuperation. "I'd be happy to come, Eli. I'd have to talk to Benjamin about using a buggy, though. It's a little cold to be walking home or taking my scooter from your house after dark. Seems like winter has come early this year."

It was true. Even though it was only early October, they'd already had several frosts. The *Farmer's Almanac* was predicting snow before Christmas and colder than usual temperatures, her stepfather, Benjamin, had told them just the other night at the supper table.

"Not to worry. I'm sure we can figure out a way to get her to and from your place," Ginger's mother assured Eli.

"A good thing to do, Ginger," Joe put in. "Helping a neighbor in need. You catch a ride in the morning or walk to Eli's, and I could give you a ride home most nights."

Ginger felt a little shiver of excitement. "You would, Joe?" She looked from him to her mother. "Isn't that nice of Joe to offer?"

"I wouldn't want to put Joe out," her mother answered, her tone cool.

Ginger frowned. She didn't know what had gotten into her mother, being almost rude to Joe.

"You wouldn't be putting me out," Joe contended. "I go right down your road most days. My uncle's put me in charge of looking in on crews, so I'm here and there all day. Not many he trusts to see the job gets done."

"It's kind of you to offer, Ginger." There was emotion in Eli's voice. "And also kind of you, Joe." He looked back at Ginger. "And if you're sure you'd like to help me, I'll accept. My children will be so excited."

"Then it's decided." Ginger's mother clasped her hands together, settling the matter. "Monday morning you say, Eli?"

"*Ya*. I have to be on the job by eight, but it's less than half an hour to the work site by buggy," Eli answered. "I'd offer to take Ginger home each night, but Lizzy can't be out and about yet, and I can't leave the children at home. I know some folks think a boy of eight is old enough to leave home alone with brothers or sisters, but I don't do it. I'd worry too much."

"You're a good father, Eli," Ginger's mother told him. "And don't you fret. We'll figure out how to get Ginger to and from." She produced her shopping list. "Well, we best be on our way. Tara's waiting on raisins."

"*Ya*, and I need to get home. Claudia's with the children, but I promised her I wouldn't be long." Eli picked up his shopping basket from the floor. "Just needed to pick up a prescription at the drugstore for Lizzy and stop for a few groceries. I've got a driver waiting. Hired a van to take Lizzy to the doctor this morning, then home, then back into town."

"Forty-nine!" a different clerk called from the deli counter. "Forty-nine!"

"Guess I'd best go get my sub before someone else does." Joe boldly met Ginger's gaze. "You going to the Fishers' Saturday night? I hear there's going to be a bonfire."

"I think so," she said, trying not to sound too excited. But if they were both there, Joe would surely offer to take her home, wouldn't he? It was the way young men and women dated among the Old Order Amish. They attended chaperoned events separately and then a boy was free to ask a girl if he could give her a ride home.

"We'll have to see," Ginger's mother responded, then turned to Eli. "Ginger will be there at seven-fifteen on Monday."

"Excellent." Eli nodded his head again and again, gripping the shopping basket in one hand. "Wonderful." He looked at Ginger. "Goodbye. Thank you again."

"You're welcome," Ginger told Eli, but her eyes were all for Joe Verkler as he walked away.

Eli entered his cozy kitchen in his stocking feet. They had an unusual rule for an Amish family—no boots or shoes in the house. They wore socks or slippers beyond the mudroom. He had made the rule after his wife, Elizabeth, died three years ago. It was the only way he had found to keep clean the hardwood floors he had so lovingly laid for her. "Guess who's home?" he sang, carrying a paper sack of groceries in each arm.

"*Dat!*"

"*Dat!*"

"*Dat!*" his three sons cried, one after the other.

The youngest, five-year-old Phillip, threw himself at his father, wrapping his arms around Eli's knees. "What did you bring us?"

"Phillip." Eli's sister, Claudia, spoke from where she stood at the stove, stirring something in a cast-iron kettle. Something that smelled deliciously of chicken and vegetables and herbs. "Don't ask such things. Offer to help your *fadder* with his bags."

"I'll get one," Eli's oldest son, eight-year-old Simon, said, taking a bag from his father's arms.

"I'll help," seven-year-old Andrew piped up.

When Andrew took the second bag from Eli, Phillip immediately grabbed it, practically knocking both of them off their feet.

"Whoa," Eli said, taking the bag from his boys and righting Andrew.

"I want to help," Phillip complained.

Andrew crossed his arms over his chest in annoyance. "You're not big enough."

"Am too!" Phillip, who looked just like Eli had as a child—bright red hair and all—gazed up at his father. "Andrew says I'm not big. But this morning you said I was big now."

Eli rumpled his son's coarse hair as he walked past him, taking the grocery sack to the table. "I *said* you're bigger than Lizzy. Which means you're responsible for her and also means you shouldn't tease her."

"I see you bought cookies." Claudia left her place at the stove and began to unload the first bag. "Plenty of cookies." She stacked the packages of them on the table. "Did you remember the rosemary?"

"*Ya.* It's in one of the bags. They didn't have fresh, but you said dry would do." Eli walked to the stove. "I don't know what you've made but it smells wonderful." He picked up a wooden spoon from the walnut countertop he'd built and stirred the thick, creamy stew in the pot.

"Chicken potpie," Claudia told him. "I just turned it off. Piecrust is already made and on the counter under the damp towel. Pour the stew into the piecrust, cover it with the second crust and be sure to vent it or you'll have a mess to clean up. Bake for forty-five minutes at three-fifty degrees. The oven is already preheating." She held a pack of Oreos in one hand and peanut butter sandwich cookies in the other. "Really, Eli," she said gently. "The children don't need all of these sweets."

"Maybe they're for me," he teased as he set down the spoon.

"Then you don't need them, either."

He laughed at the stern look on his sister's face. "They eat healthy enough. We all do. How's Lizzy?"

"Tired but good," she said, putting the packages of cookies in the pie safe that had been a gift to Eli and Elizabeth when they'd married. It had been his great-grandmother's. "I think the trip to the doctor wore her out. She should stay in bed for the rest of the day. If she wants to eat with the family, maybe carry her out to the kitchen?"

"I'll see what she wants to do. Some nights we eat with her in her room." He looked to Simon, Andrew and Phillip. "Don't we, boys?"

"Sometimes," Phillip agreed, biting on the end of a package of cookies, trying to open it with his teeth.

Simon took the bag from his little brother. "None before supper."

"*Dat!*" Phillip cried in protest.

"He's right. You shouldn't be eating cookies, Phillip." Eli turned to his sister. "Thank you so much for staying with them while I went back into town. You should go home. John will be wanting his supper soon."

"You sure?" Claudia closed the pie safe. "I can get the potpie in the oven for you."

"I can manage the potpie," Eli assured her. "Guess what?" Suddenly he couldn't hide his excitement. "I found someone to watch the children while I work that job. The one Ader Verkler wants to hire me to do."

"You did? That's wonderful news." She removed her apron and hung it on a peg on the wall. "Who?"

"Ginger Stutzman," he announced, unable to stop grinning. There was something about Ginger that made him smile every time he saw her. Yes, she could be silly and coquettish at times, but he admired her enthusiasm for life. She always had a light in her eyes that he sensed came from deep within her.

"Ginger?" Claudia made a face that left no room for interpretation. Obviously she didn't approve.

He lowered his voice, walking near to his sister so the children wouldn't hear. "What's wrong with Ginger? The children adore her."

His sister looked at him in a way that immediately made him feel a little bit as if they were back on their parents' farm in Wisconsin, and he was ten, and she was fifteen again. Their mother had died when he was eight, and at thirteen, Claudia had taken on most of the household chores so their father could continue to work their dairy farm. Her duties, among others, had been to care for Eli and their other siblings. She had not quite taken on the role of mother but embraced her new responsibilities as an older sister. Eli and Claudia had remained close, and after he lost his wife, she had become his best friend.

Claudia took a deep breath. "I'm sorry to be cross. It's just been a long day. There's nothing wrong with Ginger. She'll make an excellent sitter."

He followed her to the mudroom. "My same thought."

"I just think you need to be careful," she went on as she took her heavy wool cloak from a peg and threw it over her shoulders.

"Careful of what?"

Claudia glanced in the direction of the boys as she reached for her heavy black bonnet. Phillip had managed to get into the cookies and each boy had one stuffed in his mouth. She looked back at Eli. "She's a flirt," she said quietly.

"And?" Eli pressed. Because he knew she was a flirt. Everyone in Hickory Grove knew it. She always had been. But she was also a good person, a woman of faith, and he had never heard anyone ever speak of her behaving improperly. More importantly, he knew he could trust her with his children, who were more precious to him than anything he had on this earth.

"And I wouldn't want you to…misinterpret anything she might say or do."

He tipped back his head and laughed. Nothing could dampen his mood today. Because his problem was solved with childcare, and the money he would make would not only be enough to pay all of Lizzy's medical bills but also to buy a pony for Christmas for the children. *"Misinterpret?"*

Claudia met his gaze with green eyes. "You know very well what I'm talking about. I understand you want to marry again. I just wouldn't want you to—" She let the sentence go unfinished.

"Wouldn't want me to *what*?" he pressed.

"Fall in love with her," she said.

Eli laughed. "I'm not a boy just out of school." He

opened his arms wide. "I'm practically an old man. A woman like Ginger wouldn't be interested in me."

"That said…" Her tone softened. "You have such a big heart, Eli." She exhaled and went on. "I wouldn't want to see it broken. And Ginger Stutzman—" she tapped his chest "—will break it if you let her."

Chapter Two

Eli stood on the steps of the back porch, watching as his sister went down the driveway on her push scooter, her black cloak whipping behind her. He smiled to himself, silently giving thanks for her dedication to him and his children, and to her willingness to speak up. Even when he didn't agree with her. He wasn't offended by what she had said about Ginger or him. Her heart was in the right place.

He chuckled to himself as he entered the warm house again. Did Claudia really think he would pursue Ginger Stutzman, the prettiest, most eligible young woman in Hickory Grove? And probably eight years younger than him? Did his sister believe he would think Ginger would ever be interested in him? Women like Ginger would never give a man his age a second glance. They went for flashy young men like that Joe Verkler from Lancaster.

In the kitchen, Eli put an end to the cookie snack, asked his boys to set the table for supper and then padded down the hallway. He quietly entered the parlor in case Lizzy was sleeping. Ordinarily, they all slept upstairs, but he'd moved her downstairs so he would be closer to her during the day. He slept on the sofa on the far side of the room, just in case she needed him during the night. His boys continued to sleep upstairs, though occasionally he woke in the morning to find Phillip either sleeping at the foot of his sister's bed or snuggled in Eli's arms.

Eli's gaze settled on his daughter. She was sitting propped up on pillows in her bed, a log cabin quilt tucked around her. She was playing with the little faceless doll Ginger had made for her and a wooden horse he'd carved to go with other wooden animals his children shared.

"*Dat*!"

"Lizzy." Eli went to her and sat on the edge of her bed. "Your aunt says you're feeling pretty good?"

She nodded. Her blond hair was pulled back and covered with a white handkerchief that matched her white sleeping gown.

He smoothed the hair that had escaped from her headcovering. "But a little tired maybe?" he asked in Pennsylvania *Deitsch*.

"*Ya*." She looked up at him with her mother's big, brown, expressive eyes.

Eli swallowed hard, wrapping his arms around his daughter. She hugged him tight. "Guess what," he whispered in her ear.

"What?" she whispered back with a little giggle. "Did you bring cookies, *Dat*?"

"I did," he told her, easing her back onto her pillow. "And Jell-O and pudding. But this is better than treats.

Ginger is going to be keeping an eye on you while I go to work."

The little girl grinned. "I *wike* Ginger." Then she knitted her brows. "But why do you have to go to work, *Dat*? I'll *mish* you."

He drew the quilt up to her chin and smoothed it. "Because that's what *fadders* do. They go to work so they can buy cookies." He tickled her belly and she giggled again. "And I'll come home to you every night by dinnertime. *Ya*?"

"*Ya*," she echoed, looking up at him from beneath long lashes.

Eli had always known he would become a father someday. And he had known he would be good at it because he had helped Claudia take care of their five younger siblings after their mother's death. His childhood experiences had prepared him for the crying babies, the dirty faces and the mischievous antics of little boys. What he had not been prepared for was this sweet ache he felt deep in his chest, an ache of love for his children that was like no other feeling in the world. He would do anything for his Lizzy, for his boys. *Anything* to keep them safe and warm and cared for.

He sighed as Lizzy relaxed and closed her eyes. It hadn't been an easy row to hoe, being a single father with little ones. He constantly felt as if he was being pulled in so many directions at once. There were cows to be milked, animals to be fed, dishes to be washed and beds to be made. And then there were his responsibilities in his children's religious education. Some days it was too much for one man. That was why God joined

Adam and Eve together, so that they could go about their tasks together. He truly believed that.

Eli stroked Lizzy's forehead, thankful she was no longer burning with the fever that had plagued her on and off for weeks. She was falling asleep.

He didn't agree with what Claudia had been saying about Ginger, but she had been right in saying he wanted a wife. And he wanted a mother for his children. His children needed a mother.

Watching Lizzy's rosebud lips part as she exhaled slowly, he clasped his hands and prayed a quick, silent thank-you for God's mercy in saving his daughter from her illness. And then he prayed, as he prayed every day, for God to provide him a wife.

"I suppose we'd best get home," Ginger's twin sister, Bay, said, drying her hands on her apron. They had just pulled four loaves of fresh bread from Eli's oven, and the entire house smelled delightful. "Unless you want me to wait for you and give you a ride home." She glanced at the clock. It was five-fifteen. "I imagine Eli will be home soon."

Bay wasn't the cook Tara was, but she had the touch when it came to yeast breads. She'd come for the afternoon to help Ginger make loaves of honey-wheat sandwich bread. It had been Ginger's idea to make it, thinking the bread would serve well for the sandwiches Eli took to work every day. Usually, he just ate his sandwiches on inexpensive white bread from the grocery store. However, earlier in the week he'd gone on so much about how good the homemade sandwich bread her mother had sent for him was that she thought he ought to have a few loaves of his own. She planned to slice the bread after it cooled and freeze it on cookie sheets before putting it in plastic bags in the freezer. That way, he could quickly grab what he needed in the morning and not worry about the bread going moldy in the pie safe because, without preservatives, the home-made bread had a short shelf life.

Ginger was finishing up her second week caring for Eli's children, and so far, it had gone well. The children liked her, Lizzy was improving every day and Eli seemed thrilled to have her. The idea that she could ease another's burden, especially a man so good-hearted as Eli, made Ginger feel good in a way she'd never felt before. And Eli was so appreciative of anything she did. He always made a point of telling her how delicious the meals she left for him were and reminded her every day that he didn't expect her to cook, and certainly not clean. He kept repeating that he had hired her to care for his children. But it was no burden for Ginger. She liked cooking on her own without Tara or her mother overseeing her every move, and she was discovering she was actually a decent cook in her own right. And she enjoyed the cleaning. It gave her time to pray, and also to daydream.

These days, she was spending a lot of time day-dreaming.

After years of flirtations, Ginger was feeling more and more as if she was ready to marry, settle down and run her own household. The time she spent with Lizzy, Phillip, Andrew and Simon made her think about the possibility of having her own children. Was that why God had put Joe in her path? Because He was ready to see her as a wife and a mother? Ginger knew it wasn't wise to guess at God's intentions, but it just made sense, didn't it?

Bay's voice penetrated Ginger's thoughts, sounding impatient. Ginger had an idea her sister was repeating her question. "Do you want me to wait or no?"

Ginger looked to Bay. She was a redhead, not a blonde like Ginger was, tall, like their older sister Lovage, and willowy to Ginger's curves. They did have the same color green eyes, though.

"No need to wait," Ginger said quickly. Using the hem of her apron as a hot mitt, she slid one of the hot loaves of bread away from the edge of the stove. All it would take was one curious boy to send the bread tumbling to the floor.

"You sure?" Bay caught the hand of one of their little brothers as he ran by. "Give me that," she said. "No more cookies, Josiah. *Mam* won't be happy with us if you two have any more cookies before supper."

Josiah solemnly handed over the store-bought sweet, a bite missing from it.

Bay had brought their twin brothers with her, two-year-olds Josiah and James. Technically, they were only their half brothers. Their mother and stepfather's sons, though neither of them felt any differently about these two than their brother Jesse, who shared the same father with them.

"Where do they keep finding these cookies?" Bay asked.

Ginger laughed. "I don't know. Eli buys them. The boys squirrel them away around the house. Yesterday I found a box of animal crackers in the linen closet." She reached down and wiped the chocolate crumbs from the corner of her little brother's mouth. "Where's James?" she asked, leaning over him. "Go find James. It's time to go home."

The two sisters watched as their little brother, dressed in denim pants, shirts and suspenders, toddled out of the kitchen, calling his twin's name in a cherubic voice.

"I don't need a ride home," Ginger repeated, giving the beef stew on the back of the stove a stir. "I have one."

Bay frowned. "I suppose *he's* bringing you home again?"

Ginger felt her cheeks grow warm. "*He* has a name." She turned down the flame beneath the cast-iron pot of stew. "Joe Verkler."

Bay made a sour face, resting one hand on her hip. "I'm sorry, but I don't care for Joe."

Ginger tried not to let her feelings be hurt. "Why not? He's handsome and fun and…and he likes me."

"Everyone likes you," Bay quipped. "You can do better, Ginger. You *deserve* better."

Ginger wanted to ask Bay what she knew about young men. She'd never even had a beau. But she bit back the comment. "Why don't you like him?"

Bay arched her eyebrows as if it was a foolish question. "Because he's conceited. He thinks he's good-looking."

"You don't think he is?"

"I think there are more important things. I've seen him around. All he does is talk about himself and his accomplishments. He's got every single woman in Hickory Grove gazing up at him with starry eyes. They all listen to whatever nonsense he weaves. The other day he told Tara that he owned a farm and a hundred acres in Lancaster County. If that's true," she scoffed, "what's he doing here living here in Delaware with his aunt and uncle?"

Ginger defended him. "He's helping his uncle with his business. That's why he came. His uncle needed him. Joe is managing construction crews all over the county."

Bay crossed her arms over her chest. "You see what you want to see, Ginger. You always have. From where I stand, there's no substance behind that boy's fancy sunglasses and shoes…" She exhaled, letting her thought go unfinished.

"You sound like *Mam*," Ginger countered, refusing to be upset by her sister's words. She knew Bay was only trying to look out for her, and that mattered more than her sister being wrong. "*Mam* doesn't like him, either." She walked to the refrigerator to get butter. "Well, the both of you are going to have to get used to him because I like him. Maybe even more than like him," she added with her own stubbornness. "We've really gotten to know each other since he started giving me a ride home." She pressed her lips together, suddenly brimming with excitement. "I think he's going to ask me to walk out with him. We're practically already walking out together."

Bay rolled her eyes. "You and half the girls in the county think that."

Deciding not to respond, Ginger turned the flame on under a small cast-iron pan. She thought her sister was being ridiculous, but she didn't want to quarrel with her. What was the point? She knew Joe was sincere in his attention to her. What better way to prove it than to let Bay see it? Their *mam*, as well.

Ginger was silent as she dropped a couple of table-spoons of butter into the hot frying pan. It made a satisfying sizzle, and she grabbed a wooden spoon to stir the butter to prevent it from burning. A little flour and a few minutes of browning it, and the roux would make the perfect thickening for the stew that was made from thick chunks of beef, potatoes, onions, carrots and peas.

"Josiah! James!" Bay called in the direction of the living room, where the boys were all playing. When she got no response, she called louder, "Simon, could you bring the boys? We have to go." She returned her gaze to Ginger. "Guess we'll be on our way. If you're sure you don't want us to wait."

"No need to wait." Ginger smiled. "I'll see you in an hour."

Eli's oldest son entered the kitchen, leading a boy in each hand. It was clear James and Josiah weren't ready to go home.

"Thank you, Simon," Ginger said, whisking the flour into the butter in the frying pan. "Could you check on Lizzy? See if she's awake."

When Bay and the boys first arrived, Lizzy had joined them in the living room. Ginger had settled her on the couch with a quilt over her lap and she had played with Josiah and James for almost an hour. Lizzy had set up a barnyard of wooden animals and pieces of fencing on the couch beside her and entertained the toddlers by making animal sounds. When she had started to look tired, Ginger had carried her back to her makeshift bedroom, and the child had been asleep in minutes.

Bay led their little brothers into the mudroom off the kitchen. She took one little denim coat and handed Ginger the other, and both set to dressing the boys for the chilly, wet ride home.

"Thank you for coming over to help me with the bread," Ginger said, trying to button a wiggling James into his coat. Both boys looked like their father, like Benjamin's older sons with brown hair and doe-brown eyes.

"You didn't need any help, but you're welcome." Josiah's coat secure, Bay pulled his knit cap over his head, covering his eyes. "I'm impressed with how well you're running Eli's house in just two weeks. You remind me of *Mam* in the kitchen. You've always got a bunch of things going at the same time—stew simmering, bread baking, mending at the table and children well fed and content. And so many children. Everyone wanting something at the same time. You're so calm. And capable." She shook her head. "I could never do it." She threw up her hands. "I can't imagine having my own children. My own home. It would be a disaster."

"It *wouldn't* be a disaster," Ginger chided, handing her sister her cloak. "You're going to make a wonderful wife and mother someday. You're practically running the garden shop, what with Joshua busy making plans to build his and Phoebe's new house. Running a house and a garden shop are more alike than you think." She leaned on the doorjamb. "Do you want to take a loaf of bread home?"

"*Ne*, they're for Eli. The man needs a little meat on

his bones." Her eyes twinkled. "I'm beginning to think you might just be the one to put it there."

Ginger laughed, knitting her brows. There was something in her sister's tone of voice that she couldn't quite interpret. "And what's that supposed to mean?"

Bay shrugged. "I don't know. All afternoon I heard Eli this and Eli that. I think you might like him."

"Of course I like him." She gave her sister a little push. "But not *that* way."

The sisters were grinning at each other when Simon walked back into the mudroom. "Lizzy wants you," he announced, looking up at Ginger. He didn't look as much like Eli as Phillip did. He and Lizzy both resembled their mother more, but he was just like his father, such a caregiver. And so easygoing with his younger siblings. At least most of the time.

"See you at home," Ginger told her sister. "And you two, as well." She kissed the top of each of their little brothers' heads and made her way toward the back of the house to check on her charge. "Coming, Lizzy!"

Eli stood in the downstairs bathroom drying his face with a hand towel that was freshly washed and smelled of fabric softener. Ginger had declared Fridays washday and, despite his protests, had done all of his laundry two weeks in a row. She wouldn't listen to him when he assured her he could wash his and the children's clothes on Saturday mornings.

Before Ginger had started working for him, he'd managed the laundry. The children had always had clean clothes for the Sabbath at least, and the bedsheets and towels got washed at some point each month.

Though his towels had never smelled this good or been this soft. He smiled to himself in the mirror, then leaned over the sink, taking a closer look. When had signs of his aging appeared, he wondered, looking at the man he barely recognized. Last time he looked in the mirror, he didn't recall the gray at his temples.

He looked older than thirty-three.

But how long had it been since he'd scrutinized his appearance beyond checking to be sure he was tidy? Not since Elizabeth died, he guessed. Where had those fine lines around his mouth come from? The ones at the corners of his eyes? He would be thirty-four come spring. It seemed too young to be going gray, he thought wistfully.

He wondered what Ginger thought of his looks. Did she see the gray, too? The wrinkles?

He dismissed the thought. Vanity wasn't a positive attribute in a man his age, with his responsibilities. And as he had told his sister, a woman like Ginger, years younger than him, would never so much as look his way.

He hung the sweet-smelling towel on the hook beside the sink, took up a brush and tidied his hair. And smiled again.

Things were going so well these days that all he did was smile. Ader Verkler was well pleased with the work Eli was doing on the job site, and more importantly, life was running more smoothly at home. Mary Yoder, who had watched the children for him before she'd left the state to be wed, had certainly done a fine enough job, but Ginger was impressive. Particularly for her age. He would have thought a young girl like her would have struggled, with four little ones to keep, with just get-

ting something together for the noonday meal, but every
night, she not only had tasks around the house done,
but she made him supper. Every night he came into the
house to a warm kitchen smelling of biscuits or bread
or homemade cupcakes. And there was always a soup
or a stew or a ham ready to go on the table.

He walked out of the bathroom, still smiling. Tonight, not only had he come home to the heavenly scent
of bubbling spaghetti sauce, but his little Lizzy had
been sitting at the table buttering slices of bread to go
into the broiler. In just two weeks' time, his daughter's
strength had greatly improved, and he was certain it
was in good part due to Ginger's mothering skills and
practicality. She was so good at coddling Lizzy when
she needed to be coddled but also pushing her to help
her gain her strength back. It had never occurred to Eli
to have her do a chore at the table.

"There you are," Ginger said as he walked into the
kitchen. She dried her hands on her apron. "I have to
go. When you're ready to eat, throw the noodles into
boiling water and cook them for ten minutes or so. And
don't overcook them, Eli," she warned, pointing her
finger at him.

He smiled, walking over to the table where Lizzy
was still working on buttering the bread. He kissed the
top of her head. "You know," he teased Ginger, "I *have*
made noodles before."

Ginger flashed him a smile that lit up her entire face.

"*Ya*," she agreed. "And overcooked them, I hear."
She whipped her apron off. "Most people do. It should
still have a bit of a snap to it in the middle," she explained, tucking tendrils of blond hair beneath the dark

green scarf she wore to cover her hair. Like many young Amish women, she preferred a scarf to her prayer *kapp* when doing household chores. "Simon is outside gathering eggs, and the other two rascals are in the attic getting their clothes. With the rain, I had to hang some things up there to dry. Towels and sheets are done. I used the propane dryer. I hope that's okay."

"Of course." Eli followed her to the mudroom, hating to see her go so soon. All day he looked forward to the few minutes he would spend with Ginger before she headed home. He told himself that he was simply seeking adult conversation, but he talked to other men on the job site during the day. If he was honest with himself, it was Ginger he wanted to talk to. He'd always liked her, but since he had seen what she was capable of, how well she handled the children, he liked her even more. "You don't want to stay for supper?" he asked. "I promise I'll cook the noodles right. Al dente, I think the English call it."

She laughed. "Sorry. I have to go. Joe's waiting for me."

As if on cue, a male voice hollered her name from outside. The family dog, Molly, began to bark.

Eli made an effort not to frown, though just the thought of the young man brought a sourness to his mouth. He'd seen Joe at the house where he was working and had observed that the man didn't really know what he was doing. He talked a lot, threw orders around, but when it came down to it, he didn't know anything about laying bricks, putting on a roof or managing men. "Joe's outside, is he?"

"*Ya*," Ginger said cheerfully, throwing her black cloak over her shoulders.

Eli's brow creased. "Why doesn't he come inside when he picks you up?"

"Ginger! You coming?" Joe shouted.

Molly continued to bark. The dog Eli had raised from a pup usually liked most people. But the black-and-white shaggy mixed breed didn't like Joe Verkler. She barked like crazy every time he came up the driveway with his fancy rig. A rig Eli was certain had some kind of music player inside. He'd passed a buggy the other night on Route 8 and heard Englisher music blasting from inside. He was sure the driver had been Joe. He was also fairly certain he'd seen a young Amish woman with him. He hadn't been able to identify the woman in the dark, but the one thing he did know was that it hadn't been Ginger.

Ginger offered a quick smile as she yanked her bonnet over her head. "Joe wants to get home after a long day at work. You understand." She tied the bonnet on tightly. "I'll see you Monday morning, *ya*?"

Eli nodded as he watched her step out of the slippers she now kept at his door and into a pair of black rubber boots. It was on the tip of his tongue to ask her again to stay and have supper with them. After they ate, maybe they could play a board game, then he could load up all of the children, and they would take her home.

But that wasn't practical, of course. Lizzy didn't need to be outside at night. And why would Ginger want to sit and have a boring family dinner and talk about the dogwood flowers he was carving into a piece of wood, or what kind of spider his boys had found, when she could spend time with an exciting man like Joe.

Joe's voice came through the door as she opened it. "Ginger! I'm leaving with or without you!"

"Coming!" Ginger shouted.

Eli held open the door to the back porch. "*Ya*, I'll see you Monday," he agreed. Then he watched Ginger cut across the wet porch and tried to keep from counting the hours until he saw her again.

Chapter Three

Ginger sat on the top step of Eli's porch a week later tossing a stick for the family's black-and-white dog to fetch. Molly took off across the grass that had gone brown with the cooler weather, and Ginger's gaze strayed to the county road in the distance. A red pickup truck flew past Eli's mailbox, but there was no sign of the two-seated buggy she was looking for.

She sighed. Joe was late to pick her up and take her home.

Molly ran to the steps and dropped the stick at Ginger's feet. When Ginger didn't pick it up, the dog gave a subdued woof.

Ginger scratched the shaggy black-and-white dog's head. "Go away. I don't want to play anymore."

The dog put one paw and then the other on the bottom step, pushing the stick closer. Ginger remembered when Eli had found the dog as a puppy in a cardboard box in the parking lot of Byler's store. Abandoned. Eli had brought it home, bottle-fed the pup goat's milk and named her Molly when he knew she was going to make it. She was such a well-behaved dog that Ginger wondered if Molly sensed what a good life she had on the Kutz farm and wanted to express her appreciation.

Molly whined and pushed the stick at Ginger again.

Ginger laughed. "All right. Just once more." She tossed the stick, and the dog took off as the screen door opened and closed behind her.

It was Andrew, Eli's middle son. He was a sweet, thoughtful boy with a mop of reddish-blond hair and a pair of round wire-frame glasses that made him look older than his seven-going-on-eight years. "*Dat* says you should come back inside," he said in Pennsylvania *Deitsch*.

"I'm waiting for my ride home," she explained.

Molly raced up to the steps again, stick in her mouth, and Andrew accepted it from her and threw it hard. It landed on the far side of the driveway, and the dog took off after it.

"Getting cold out," Andrew said, shoving his hands deep into his pockets, something his father often did. "It's warm in the kitchen."

Ginger smiled up at him from her perch on the top step. "I'm fine. I'm sure Joe will be here any minute. He's in charge of a lot of men. He can't just quit at four like your *dat*." This was the second time Joe had been late that week. When he'd been late last time, he'd spent the entire ride home explaining to her how central he was to his uncle's entire construction business. Still, she felt as if she was making an excuse for Joe when she said it aloud.

The boy wandered back into the house. A minute later, the screen door opened and closed shut again.

"I sent Andrew out to get you."

Ginger looked up to see Eli. He had washed his face as he did every day after he returned home from work, and she could see that his hair was damp at the temples. It was an auburn color, darker than her sister Bay's or Tara's red hair, and he kept it well trimmed. She liked that. "Joe's running late. A problem at one of the job sites, I'm sure," she said.

Eli slid his hands into his pants pockets and gazed out at the barnyard.

It was a small farm, maybe twenty-five acres, with a neat little two-story square bungalow with a wide porch along the driveway side. The yard comprised a series of standard Amish outbuildings: a dairy barn, a lean-to shed for farm equipment, a windmill, a chicken house and a woodshed. Everything was painted, neat and orderly. What was interesting to Ginger about the property was that unlike most Amish houses, which were painted white, his was a spruce green. Not *Plain*, but not too fancy, either.

Ginger pressed her lips together. She didn't often wish for Englisher conveniences, but it was times like this that she almost wished she had a cell phone. Then Joe could have let her know he was going to be late. That he'd gotten held up. Most Amish families in Hickory Grove had a cell phone these days. However, they were only used for emergencies, or when someone worked for Englishers and had to check in with their boss. Her mother and stepfather didn't have a cell at their house because there was a phone in the harness shop.

"Starting to rain again," Eli remarked. "Might turn to sleet. Why don't you wait inside with us?"

She tightened her heavy cloak around her. She *was* getting cold. And she was disappointed that Joe was late again. It would be dark soon. She watched Molly for a moment. The dog had grown bored with the game of fetch and was now digging at the base of a big silver maple tree that, in the summer, shaded the porch. She gazed up at Eli.

He tipped his head in the direction of the back door. "Come on," he coaxed. "You can wait inside for him where it's warm as easily as you can sit out here in the cold."

He had a gentle way about him. A calmness that made Ginger feel like… Like everything was going to be all right. Always.

"Lizzy just woke up and she was disappointed you were gone," Eli continued. "She'd be tickled to see you."

Ginger rose, looked in the direction of the road once more, then followed Eli into the house. The fragrant smell of the roast beef she'd left in the oven hit her the moment she stepped into the mudroom. She removed her coat and bonnet, stepped out of her rubber boots and into the spare slippers she kept there now. At first, she had thought it odd that Eli didn't allow shoes inside his house, but now she liked the idea. It kept the floors so much cleaner that she was thinking maybe once she and Joe were married, she'd establish the same rule in her home. She'd set a bench in the mudroom just like Eli had, and when Joe came home from work, he could sit on the bench, remove his barn boots and slip into a pair of cozy slippers she would make for him.

The daydream made her smile.

"Ginger!" Lizzy cried the moment Ginger stepped

into the kitchen. "I thought you was gone." The little girl was seated at one end of the kitchen table with a basket of fabric scraps and buttons. She was sewing little bits of fabric together the way Ginger had shown her, the same way Ginger's mother had taught her a very long time ago. "Look, *it'sh* me." She held up a rectangle of fabric two inches tall with a yellow button sewn on for a head.

"It is!" Ginger agreed.

On the far end of the kitchen table was a brightly colored tin Chinese checkers board, all set for two players. Andrew was leaning against the table, playing with an old hinge he'd found outside.

"You want to play?" Ginger asked him, pointing at the game.

Andrew made a face. "Nah."

"You like Chinese checkers?" Eli asked Ginger, looking surprised.

"I love it."

"I'll play you then. I love the game, too. I know it's simple. More of a child's game, but—" He shrugged. He was standing at the stove, stirring the succotash Ginger had put on. "I played it with my *dat* many a night, even when I was no longer a boy."

"I used to play with my *dat* all the time, too." The memory made her smile. He'd been gone five years now. "We took turns playing him, my sisters and me. No one could beat him but me. Though that didn't happen often," she admitted.

"I was always pretty good myself." He walked toward the table, drying his hands on a dish towel. "Let's see if I can beat you."

She glanced at the stove. "The roast should be ready in half an hour or so. The potatoes should—"

"Just turned them on," he said, sliding into the chair at the head of the table where the board was set up. He tapped the chair to his right. "Come on. It'll be fun."

Eli smiled at Ginger across the round, colorful tin board that looked old and well loved. Bought new, the game board sometimes contained pegs instead of marbles. This one was marbles— red and green—set up in triangles across from each other. "You go first."

She took the chair. She had been on the verge of falling into a sour mood due to Joe's tardiness, but now she was smiling. "You sure you want to play me? You won't be embarrassed in front of your daughter, will you?" She indicated Lizzy, who was engrossed with her sewing.

He made a face at Ginger. "Why would I be embarrassed?"

She laughed. "When I beat you." And then she took her turn.

Ginger didn't beat Eli on the first game, but she did the second. They laughed and chatted while playing, taking turns getting up to check the potatoes and the succotash bubbling on the stove. Eli told her a funny story about one of the boys, sixteen years old and new to the building crew, who had played a practical joke on the father, who was also on the crew. The boy had opened their lunch boxes and passed his father a sandwich made with chocolate chip cookies between the slices of bread instead of meat and cheese. The joke had been on the boy because his father had eaten every bite, remarking how good the sandwich was. And Ginger had told Eli about her twin sister, Bay's growing greenhouse and garden shop business. Bay had started it with Benjamin's son Joshua, and even though there were other greenhouses in the area, their customers were increasing each week. They were planning to have a Christmas shop this year selling fresh-picked greenery and homemade wreaths and garlands, and were even going to give a workshop on how to make a fresh wreath.

"We should play again," Eli dared when they finished the second game and were tied.

"Supper is ready." She pointed to the stove. The roast was resting on the stovetop. They'd prepared the potatoes together between turns at the game board. Eli had mashed; she had added just the right amount of buttermilk and salt.

"Supper can wait," Eli told Ginger. He glanced at Lizzy, still sitting at the other end of the table, busy with her scraps of fabric.

"The children are hungry," Ginger argued.

"They're not hungry. I bet they ate cookies all day." He looked at his daughter. "Lizzy, you're not hungry, are you?"

The three-year-old looked up from her project. "*Ya.* I want *potatoesh.* I'm tired of *shoup.*"

Ginger raised her brows at Eli as if to say "I told you so."

"Then you should eat with us, Ginger." He got up from the table, taking the checkerboard with him. "And I won't take no for an answer. You made enough roast beef for two suppers."

"The extra is for you to pack for lunch tomorrow."

"Still too much," he noted. "I can't eat an entire roast

for lunch. I'd be napping away the afternoon instead of working."

Ginger chuckled as she checked the clock on the wall. Joe was almost two hours late. She glanced out the window. And it was dark now. She wasn't sure what to do: start walking home, have something to eat and wait or—

The unmistakable sound of hoofbeats and buggy wheels came from outside and was immediately joined by the sound of Molly barking.

"He's here! I best go." Ginger leaped up from the chair and hurried to put on her boots and cloak. "It was fun to play checkers," she called over her shoulder.

Eli offered a quick smile and then turned to the stove. "*Ya.* See you tomorrow."

Something in the sound of his voice made her turn back to look at him. His gaze met hers, and he held it for a moment. The way he was looking at her made her feel strange. Strange but not uncomfortable. There was…a warmth in his gaze. "See you tomorrow," she repeated. Then she hurried outside, putting a bright smile on her face. "Joe!" she called to him. Feeling somehow upended, she didn't look back at the house, even though she knew Eli was standing in the doorway, watching her go.

On a Thursday just after noon, Ginger put the finishing touches on the wedding table called the *eck*, where her newly married friends Mary Lewis and Caleb Gruber would share their first meal as man and wife. It was the Amish tradition for a woman to marry in her parents' home, but there were so many wedding guests, Mary's family had transformed the family's barn into a beautiful dining room. They had swept and scrubbed the cement floor until it was as clean as a kitchen floor. Then they had hung white bedsheets to hide the barn walls and stalls and they'd set up more than a dozen tables and covered them with fine tablecloths. Benches and chairs had been added to seat a hundred and fifty guests, and then the whole makeshift room had been transformed with white china and colored glass dishware, bales of straw, pumpkins and vases of fall grasses and leaves. Ginger and the other single girls had adorned the *eck* not just with miniature white and orange pumpkins and mums and marigolds, but also with paper hearts as well as vases of celery, which was an Amish tradition. And now that the wedding ceremony was over and Mary and Caleb were wed, the traditional dinner would be served.

The ceremony had been typical for Kent County Old Order Amish with a three-hour morning church service. Preacher Barnabas, Caleb's father, had given a long sermon based on the book of Tobit, which had always been one of Ginger's favorite books of the Bible. The sermon was followed by hymns sung by wedding guests while Mary and Caleb met alone with the bishop for last-minute scriptural and personal words of wisdom. Then the couple had joined the congregation and made their vows, before friends and family, to care for each other and remain faithful until death parted them. The wedding ceremony ended with the couple and the guests kneeling for a final prayer led by Mary's bishop. And now everyone was ready to celebrate with the wedding dinner, which would be followed by more singing, visiting, matchmaking and the bride and groom opening their gifts. The day would wrap up with a wedding supper for a smaller crowd.

It was a big wedding with not only family and friends attending from Hickory Grove and Rose Valley, but from as far away as Kansas and Kentucky. With the ceremony complete, the women were now preparing to put on the midday meal. There would be roast chicken and beef, mashed potatoes and gravy, cabbage, dinner rolls, canned pears, canned peaches and Jell-O salads. And of course no Amish wedding dinner was complete without the traditional creamed celery dish.

As Ginger put a finishing touch on a garland of wheat sheaves draped across the front of the *eck*, she spotted Joe. He was standing in a knot of young, unmarried men, all in their twenties. Her stepbrother Levi was among them. Levi, who was home visiting from Lancaster County, where he was serving an apprenticeship as a buggy maker, had stood up with Caleb during the wedding ceremony. He and Mary's friend Alma, who also stood up with the couple, would join the newlyweds at the *eck*.

Like all of the weddings Ginger had attended, the ceremony had been solemn and beautiful in its simplicity. In his final comments, the bishop had emphasized the unbreakable holy bond created by marriage and the importance of this bond, not only to the couple but to the entire church community.

Ginger stood there at the bride and groom's table for a moment, hoping Joe would notice her. When he didn't, she waved at him, trying inconspicuously to get his attention.

Levi caught Ginger's eye and knitted his eyebrows questioningly. It was apparent he didn't approve of her behavior.

Ginger returned her attention to the table, straightening the silverware and wondering what he knew about her and Joe. The previous night, when Levi had arrived home, their sister Tara had chewed his ear off, telling him all of the news in Hickory Grove, and Ginger was certain she had heard her name spoken. She hoped she would get a chance to talk to Levi alone before he returned to Lancaster on Saturday. Levi had dated quite a bit since he moved to Pennsylvania, so she was hoping he might have some advice to give her as to how to navigate her relationship with Joe. She didn't want to be forward, but she also wanted to make it clear to Joe that she was a good girl and that her intention in dating him was to look toward a public courtship and then marriage.

Ginger's gaze fell on Joe, and she waved again. This time he saw her. She smiled the way she knew boys liked to be smiled at. Then she looked around to be sure her mother wasn't watching her, because if she was, she'd have something to say about Ginger being too flirty. The day before, while baking noodle casseroles to bring to the wedding, her mother had made an offhand remark about how if a girl had to chase a boy, chances were, he didn't want to be caught. She hadn't said it directly to Ginger, but Ginger had known the comment was meant for her.

Luckily, her mother was nowhere in sight. She was probably up at the house, helping Mary's aunts prepare the wedding dinner. Ginger had offered to help in the kitchen, but the aunts had sent her and several other unmarried girls away, telling them this was the time to socialize with wedding guests. "Never know when there might be another groom in the crowd," Mary's aunt Dorcas had said with a giggle.

At last, Joe acknowledged Ginger with a nod. He said something to the other men in the group and then slowly made his way around two tables to where she was standing at the *eck*. He was dressed similarly to the other male wedding guests: black pants and shirt-waist; white, long sleeve shirt; and clean black shoes. But he was so handsome that he stood out among the Kent County boys like a glittering diamond in a sack of acorns.

Standing in front of the *eck*, watching Joe walk toward her, Ginger thought dreamily of her own wedding and *eck*. She imagined sitting at the table beside Joe, sharing dinner, laughing with her guests and holding Joe's hand under the table. Everyone would comment on how perfect they were for each other and what a handsome couple they made. She wondered how big a wedding it would be. Would they invite a lot of guests, or would they make it a quieter affair? Would they go straight to Lancaster to set up housekeeping at Joe's house, or would they hire a van and go visiting, as many newlyweds did before setting up their home, staying with friends and relatives as far away as California or Canada?

"Nice service," Ginger said to Joe. "A hundred and fifty guests."

"*Ya*." Joe took a toothpick from a tiny crock on the *eck* and thrust it between his teeth.

Her first impulse was to chastise him. He wasn't supposed to be taking things from the *eck*. It was bad manners. But she held her tongue, reminding herself that rules were different in Lancaster.

Rather than looking at her, Joe's gaze wandered over the crowd as he spoke. "Not as big as the weddings we have in Lancaster. Last year, we had four hundred for my sister Trudy's wedding. We put up a kitchen tent to make all of the food."

"So you like a big wedding?" she asked, gazing up at him with a smile. He was freshly shaven, and if she didn't know better, she would have thought she smelled cologne on him. Amish men and women didn't wear colognes or perfumes. But that didn't mean a young man, thinking himself still in his *rumspringa*, didn't cross such a small line—especially one who hadn't been baptized, like Joe. During a young man's or woman's *rumspringa,* parents and elders allowed a certain amount of freedom.

"We roasted two pigs in a pit in our yard," he told her, his gaze still drifting to the crowd. "I stayed up all night, keeping the fire going. My *mam* said she couldn't have done it without me. Folks said it was the best wedding dinner they'd ever attended, on account of those pigs."

"Pigs in a hole in the ground?" Ginger asked, half thinking he was pulling her leg. "I've never heard of such a thing. Your *mam* cooked them that way?"

Joe looked down at her. "Dug a big hole, lined it with rocks and put the pigs in the hole and covered it up with rocks and dirt. The fire over it heated the rocks, which cooked the pork."

She laughed at the idea of it. "Did it take a long time?"

Again, his gaze strayed, this time fixing on something or someone over her right shoulder. "Like I said, all night. I don't know what time we put them on. Probably roasted those hogs eighteen hours or so."

Wondering what he was looking at, she glanced over her shoulder. Two rows of tables behind her stood a group of unmarried young women. Girls Ginger didn't know, probably the Grubers' relatives from elsewhere. Weddings were always a good way for unmarried young men and women to meet potential husbands and wives.

Ginger looked back at Joe, shifting her stance so she blocked his view of the young women who were now giggling openly in his direction. "You think you'll be able to give me a ride home tomorrow?" she asked. "From Eli's? I know you said you might—"

"Not sure where my uncle needs me," he interrupted. "I might be at our building site closer to Hartly."

She pressed her lips together. "So… I should wait for you or what?" Against her will, her tone turned a bit sharp.

Joe looked down at her.

Ginger couldn't read his face, and she suddenly wondered why she was pursuing him at all. Did he really have feelings for her, or did he just like being seen with her? Shouldn't *he* have been the one to initiate conversation today? Shouldn't *he* have been looking for her amongst the guests instead of the other way around? "Joe." She lowered her voice for fear someone might hear her. "I thought you said you liked me," she said boldly.

"I do, Ginger. I do."

He met her gaze, his hazel eyes for her alone at last. And she felt like she was melting.

She pressed her lips together, not sure she wanted to go on now. "You said I was the girl for you. You told me we make the perfect couple."

"We do."

He winked at her and she felt her face flush.

"Hey, Joe," one of the young men in the group called to him. "Want to head out to the fence?" He tilted his head meaningfully in the direction of the open barn doors.

Though it was late October, they had been blessed with a sunny day in the high fifties. The air was crisp but comfortable, and thankfully the clouds were light and fluffy with no sign of rain. As soon as the ceremony was over, most of the men and many of the children had moved into the barnyard to give the women room to set up the meal.

"Gotta go," Joe told Ginger, a boyish smirk on his face. "The guys need me to uh…help them out with something."

She chuckled and nodded, knowing very well what Joe and his friends were up to. It was an old tradition that young men liked to chase down the new groom and throw him over a fence. It was all in good fun and symbolized that the groom had gone from being a part of the single men to the married men. Sometimes these days, even the bride might be tossed over the fence, as well.

"I'll see you later?" she called after Joe.

He raised his hand but didn't look back at her.

Ginger watched Joe go, her gaze lingering on his

broad back and golden hair. He joined the other men, and together, they all made their way toward the barnyard. She was just about to return to the *eck* when she saw Eli. He was standing on the far side of the barn at the buffet table, a covered casserole dish in his arms. Usually, dinner was served family style, but Mary, seeing herself as a modern bride, had insisted on a buffet table. Her mother, wanting her daughter's wedding day to be right in every way, had agreed.

Eli waved at her, motioning her toward him, and smiled. She waved back. Beside him stood Lizzy. It was her first social outing since her illness.

When Lizzy waved, bouncing on her feet, Ginger felt an enormous sense of relief. Lizzy was going to be okay. Ginger couldn't imagine what Eli had gone through worrying about his daughter, feeling the weight of responsibility for an ill child while still doing all of the other tasks he had to do to care for his other children.

"Ginger!" Lizzy called.

Ginger gave the *eck* one last look, deemed it beautiful and made her way around the tables and people.

Lizzy threw her arms out, and Ginger gave her a hug. Some families weren't demonstrative in their love for their children, but from what Ginger had witnessed in Eli's home, she knew he saw nothing wrong with physical signs of affection. The little girl clung to her for a long moment, and a feeling of joy enveloped Ginger.

"You didn't come and make us *breakfasht*," Lizzy said as Ginger lowered her to the floor.

"Because today we came here to celebrate Mary and Caleb's wedding."

"I know," Lizzy said, frowning. "But I *wash* hungry, Ginger."

Ginger chuckled and looked to Eli. "I imagine you still had breakfast. What did your *dat* make you?"

Again, the frown. "He made *eggsh* but I don't like *eggsh*. I like *pancakesh*. *Boo-berry*. I like your *pancakesh*, Ginger."

Eli shook his head ever so slightly. "I made scrambled eggs and cheese. And bacon and toast," he defended.

"I like *pancakesh* with *boo-berriesh*," Lizzy repeated.

"Well, maybe I'll make blueberry pancakes tomorrow," Ginger told her. "And if you feel up to it, maybe you could even help me." She gave Lizzy's prayer *kapp* string a little tug. The little girl was dressed in a rose-colored dress and white cape, with a white prayer *kapp* that was identical to Ginger's. Ginger wondered if Eli starched her *kapp,* or if that was something his sister did for him. "How would that be?" she asked.

Lizzy's smile was enormous. "I would like that."

Ginger turned to see Eli looking down at the buffet table, which went on for twenty feet. "Is there a dessert table, or should I just put this here?" he asked.

"What did you bring?" Ginger took a look and thought, *How kind of him. No other single man brought a dish.* "You know you didn't have to."

Eli shrugged.

"Ginger," Lizzy giggled. "We made worm pudding."

Ginger opened her eyes wide. "Worm pudding?" she declared with great exaggeration.

Lizzy giggled behind her hand. "Not real *wormsh*."

She walked to her father. "They're candy *wormsh*." She pointed, almost poking her finger into the pudding. *"Shee?"*

"Candy worms?" Ginger raised her brows, looking to Eli.

He shrugged with a smile. "A tradition in our family." He pulled off the tinfoil from the pretty cut glass dish. Instead of the fruit salad or marshmallow salad one would have expected in such a delicate serving dish, the bowl was full of chocolate pudding covered in something that looked remarkably like dirt. Colored candy worms poked out of the "dirt."

"Are those real worms?" Ginger exclaimed, pretending she was afraid.

"Ne." Lizzy was still giggling. "I told you. Gummy *wormsh*!"

"Gummy worms?" Ginger glanced at Eli. His blue eyes were dancing. She returned her gaze to his daughter. "And real dirt?"

"Ne. Cookiesh. Dat crumbled *cookiesh* with a rolling pin. He let me help."

"Oh," Ginger said, still being silly. "I'm so glad, because I don't like dirt in my pudding."

Just then, one of Mary Gruber's younger sisters approached them. "Want to play with us, Lizzy?" ten-year-old Ann asked in Pennsylvania *Deitsch*.

Lizzy looked to her father for permission.

Eli hesitated, studying his daughter carefully. "You don't want to have a little rest? We can go inside. I'm sure Eunice won't mind if you lay down upstairs for a few minutes."

"I don't want to *shleep*," Lizzy pouted. "I want to play."

Eli hesitated, then gave a nod. "Okay. Go play, but if you get cold or tired or—"

"I won't," Lizzy said, accepting Ann's hand.

"I'll watch her," Ann told Eli solemnly. She was a thin girl, tall for her age, who wore round wire-frame glasses just like Eli's son Andrew.

Eli and Ginger stood side by side, watching Ann Gruber lead Lizzy to a corner of the barn where several little girls were playing with faceless cloth dolls on a bale of straw covered in fabric, which was meant to serve as extra seating.

Ginger looked at Eli and then the pretty glass bowl he had brought. "Worm pudding?"

He smiled. "Like I said. A tradition in our family. And fun. Right?" He turned back to the table. "I think I'll put it here with the salads. A person shouldn't have to wait for worm pudding until dessert."

She smiled. Practical jokes were often part of Amish weddings: a mousetrap in a salad, coffee that's been colored blue with food dye. "Oreo cookies for the dirt?" she asked.

"*Ya.* I just scrape the cream out of the middle."

"Ah, smart," Ginger told him. Then she turned, her arms crossed in front of her, to gaze out at the room. Joe hadn't come back into the barn.

"You going to join Joe for dinner?" Eli asked, shifting salads on the table to make room for his bowl.

She glanced at him. "Um… I don't know." While men and women tended to eat separately at large meals, especially if there was more than one seating, it was tradition that unmarried men and women paired off for the afternoon. Often the bride and groom got involved in the matchmaking. The couples ate together and then spent time visiting, getting to know each other. "Maybe."

Eli scowled. "Joe hasn't asked you?"

Chapter Four

The moment the words came out of Eli's mouth, he wished he could have taken them back. What did he care if Ginger ate with Joe Verkler? Everyone knew that a wedding was the perfect place for young, unmarried men and women to get to know each other within the guidelines established by the church. There were chaperones everywhere: parents, grandparents, children. Even a bishop or two. It was common practice for families with sons and daughters of marrying age to attend out-of-town weddings in the hopes they might meet the right young man or woman. Eli and his Elizabeth had met at a wedding in Lancaster. He had been a friend of the groom and she a friend of the bride. They had both been servers as they were called there and had sat together at the *eck*. They'd talked all day and into the night. It was love at first sight for Eli. And a few months later, he and Elizabeth had been sitting at their own *eck*.

Eli's gaze met Ginger's, bringing him back to the present, leaving the past behind. He knew very well why he cared if Ginger was eating with Joe. Because he didn't want to see her heartbroken. Because Ginger deserved better than Joe. That thought had been going through his head for weeks now. In Eli's opinion, Joe didn't show Ginger the respect a man ought to show a woman he supposedly cared for. And it wasn't just that he didn't pick her up from work on time.

Ginger was under the impression that she was the only woman Joe was walking out with, but Eli had heard Joe talking with other single men on the job. Joe was a popular man among the unmarried women of Kent County. He was so popular that some of the fathers Eli worked beside were complaining about him, saying he was nothing but a flirt and that they didn't trust him with their daughters. From what Eli gathered, the older men believed Joe was too flashy, too boastful and possibly not as honest as he should be.

Eli didn't know the boy well enough to make those observations, and he tried hard not to make judgments. What he *did* know, based on what he saw with his own eyes, was that Joe wasn't reliable. He'd tell Ginger he'd pick her up at five o'clock and then he'd be late. He'd begun arriving late to pick up Ginger after work so regularly that most evenings, she and Eli had time to play a game or two of Chinese checkers while supper cooked on the stove. It had become a ritual of sorts with them. Eli would arrive home from work, wash and instead of going outside to start feeding his livestock, he'd spend a little time with Ginger. And the children, of course. Most days, though, his little ones said hello and then wandered off to do whatever they'd been doing before he came home. Since Ginger had been caring for his children, they had become more independent, less clingy, particularly Lizzy. Before Ginger started working for him, some days it had been hard for him to get any work done at all because Lizzy wanted him beside her every waking moment. Perhaps some of that had to do with her illness, but he'd been seeing that behavior before she became sick.

Not only did the children enjoy Ginger's company, but so did Eli. That time he spent with Ginger each day had become one of his favorite parts of his weekday routine. It was time when he could talk a bit about his day with another adult and just relax before he started the endless list of chores that would take him straight through until bedtime.

Eli fussed with the serving bowl of pudding on the buffet, feeling awkward. He shouldn't have mentioned Joe to Ginger. It wasn't his business.

Ginger hesitated, then said under her breath, "You saw me trying to get his attention? Did anyone else see me?"

He shook his head. "I don't think so." He hesitated. He wanted to tell her what he thought. That she was too smart for Joe Verkler. Too mature. In so many ways, Joe seemed like a boy, and Ginger was a woman. Had Eli been in Joe's shoes, he'd have never been late to pick her up. He'd spend time with her every chance he got. And he certainly wouldn't be seeing other women.

Ginger held his gaze. She had green eyes with specks of brown and a sprinkling of freckles across her nose and cheeks. She was a beautiful woman for sure; she had a reputation for being one of the prettiest girls in Kent County with her blond hair and pert nose. But to

Eli, her beauty went beyond the physical. It was her spirit he found even more beautiful. It was easy to speak of one's faith, but far more challenging to live it, and Ginger lived it so well that she brought joy to others.

To him.

It crossed Eli's mind to ask her if she'd like to join *him* for the wedding dinner. Instead of sitting with the married men as he usually did, he and Ginger could sit together at one of the singles' tables. With so many people, he doubted most people would even notice. Of course, most of the single folks were younger than he was, but his community expected him to remarry, which technically meant the same freedoms allowed to younger singles applied to him as a widower.

It was just on the tip of Eli's tongue to ask Ginger to join him for the meal when her sister hurried toward the table, her *kapp* strings flying.

"There you are!" Tara bustled toward them, carrying a cast-iron Dutch oven. Like all of the Stutzman girls, nineteen-year-old Tara was pretty. She had Ginger's green eyes, but her hair was redder than her big sister's. "*Mam*'s looking for you. Something about the blue baking dish of noodle *kuchen* missing?"

Ginger knit her brows. "Oh dear. I asked Jacob to carry it to the buggy before we left home this morning. I hope we didn't leave it. It was packed in one of *Mam*'s baskets."

"I don't know anything about that, *Schweschder*," Tara said. "Our mother asked me to tell you she was looking for you if I saw you. I guess she found the green dish, but not the blue."

"Here, let me make room for you." Knowing the

pot had to be heavy, Eli started moving serving dishes around on the table to make room for the Dutch oven Tara was holding.

Tara offered a quick smile of thanks.

Eli had liked the Miller/Stutzman family the first day they had come to Hickory Grove. Benjamin and Rosemary had done something few families ever did so well, and he admired them greatly for it. Having lost their spouses of many years, they had married and somehow figured out a way to successfully blend their families. Besides Rosemary's youngest, Jesse, their ten children still living at home hadn't been little ones when they'd married. Eli knew it couldn't have been easy. But despite the many personalities and wants and needs of the household, Benjamin and Rosemary had managed to create a happy family that lived and thrived harmoniously. Not that everything always ran perfectly smoothly, but that was life, wasn't it? What mattered was that Benjamin and Rosemary were dedicated to their family, just as God meant them to be, and it showed not just in their words, but in how they carried themselves. They were some of the best role models he knew in Hickory Grove.

Ginger glanced in the direction of the doors that opened into the barnyard. "I guess I best go see what *Mam* needs," she said. She looked back at Eli. "See you tomorrow?"

"Tomorrow. But it's just a half a day. I'll be home by one. The boss is giving everyone part of the day off because of the wedding. I guess there's a bonfire or something tomorrow."

A smile lit up her face, a smile that made him warm

inside. "There is," Ginger said. "I thought I'd just have to go late. There's going to be a couple of games of *eck balle* before the meal if the weather cooperates."

"*Eck* ball, you say?" He'd heard of the game, but not seen it. It was something like dodgeball, only a small leather ball was used. The game field was a square covered in straw to cushion the players' falls, which inevitably took place.

"Levi said they play it all the time in Fivepointville, where he lives in Lancaster County."

"I'm surprised you and your friends would agree to such a thing. Girls don't usually play, do they?"

"That's why we're playing softball after the *eck balle* game," she explained. "Boys against girls. And then there's a bonfire and picnic supper. I think Mary's mother spent so much time working on the barn, they want us to use it."

"Ah. Well, if you need a ride over here." He shrugged. "I probably need to run to Byler's for groceries, anyway."

"Let me talk to *Mam*. I'm sure Tara and Nettie are going. Maybe Bay. We might just take one of the buggies." She began to back up, still talking. "I best go—" she opened her eyes wide "—and solve the mystery of the missing noodle *kuchen*."

A moment later, the Stutzman sisters were gone, and Eli stood at the buffet table, his tinfoil still in his hand, feeling foolish. Cowardly. He should have asked her. Then he thought about what he had seen from across the room—the way Ginger had looked at Joe. More importantly, the way Joe had *not* looked at her. He wondered if maybe he should pull Joe aside and tell him that if he was honestly interested in Ginger, he ought to act like it. And if he wasn't interested in her, he ought to be man enough to speak up and tell her so.

It was a ridiculous idea, of course. Eli knew that. Who was he to say such a thing to Joe? It wasn't his place.

He scanned the beautifully decorated room that was barely recognizable as a barn unless one looked up to see the rafters. It was a wonder what the women had done with pumpkins and wheat sheaves and such for decorations. The place didn't even smell like a barn, thanks to the small dishes of ground cinnamon, nutmeg, cloves and dried orange peel scattered on the tables. And the corner table where the bride and groom would soon sit was as pretty as any he had ever seen. He had the feeling that Ginger had played a part in making the *eck* so beautiful with such simple objects as colored glass dishes and jelly jars of celery.

The barn was beginning to fill with guests in anticipation of the meal that would soon be served. Amish men and women, as well as a few English folks, laughed and talked while children darted around, playing games. He thought maybe he would take a walk outside, see if he could catch a glimpse of his boys who were, hopefully, not up to no good, and then maybe join the men standing at the fence talking about what men talked about—crops and weather.

"Not the worm pudding again, Eli?"

Eli startled and turned around to see his sister behind him. Had she seen him talking to Ginger? "The children like it, Claudia," he explained. "We made two dishes. One to bring and one for home."

"You spoil them," she told him, crossing her arms. She was tall for a woman, and slender, even though she'd given birth to seven children. But Claudia was still pretty, he thought. With every passing year, she looked more like their mother, who had been just Claudia's age now when they had lost her.

"I saw you talking with Ginger."

Caught. He didn't say anything.

She sighed, gazing out over the room. He could hear her disapproval in her exhalation of breath. "I want you to meet someone. Her name is Elsie Swartzentruber. Widowed a year now. With only one child," she added, as if that would make Elsie more appealing to him. She was always trying to set him up with women. Women who didn't interest him.

Eli lowered his head. *"Claudia."* He drew out her name.

"Eli." She spoke his name the way he had spoken hers. "She's nice. And a faithful woman. And…*nice*," she repeated as if she could think of nothing else to say.

"I don't need my sister to introduce me to women," he said, walking away from her to add the foil to a pile at the end of the table so it could be reused.

"I think you do." She followed him, whispering so no one else would hear them. "Elsie is a suitable match. Only thirty-six her last birthday. Old enough to have some sense but still young enough to have more children. She's here with Josiah Yoder, from Seven Poplars. He's her brother. Come say hello. She has a nice farm in Ohio. Big, I hear."

"Claudia, I have a farm of my own. I'm not moving to Ohio."

"I'm sure Elsie would be willing to move to Delaware. Then she'd be closer to her brother and his family."

"Elsie doesn't need to move here because I'm not marrying her. I'm not walking out with her." He added the folded piece of tinfoil to the pile and turned to his sister. "I'm not even going to meet her. I'm going to go outside—" he pointed toward the open doors "—and seek the company of men. Men who won't be trying to marry me off to Elsie Yoder."

"Swartzentruber," Claudia corrected.

Eli walked past his sister and out into the cool autumn air. He wished Claudia would stop trying to set him up. He also wished he'd had the courage to ask Ginger to sit with him. Or the good sense to know his attraction to her wasn't going to go anywhere.

"A perfect match, Mary and Caleb," Atarah remarked to Ginger as she pulled hot dogs out of a package and placed them on a platter. She was one of Mary's cousins from Kentucky, chubby and towheaded, with thick glasses, a pointed chin and a sweet disposition. "And such a fun wedding supper last night. I laughed and laughed when Mary had Caleb open the wedding gift from our uncle, and the plastic spider popped out." She began to chuckle. "I've never seen Caleb move so fast!"

Ginger smiled as she busied herself beside Atarah at the kitchen counter. The Amish loved practical jokes, but apparently, Mary's family *really* loved them. There had also been a gift of a mixing bowl full of felt mice.

A group of friends and family were gathered in Mary's mother's kitchen, preparing snacks and supper for the bonfire frolic. Mary's parents had gone visiting for the day to allow the young people to enjoy themselves without an older member of the community dampening their fun. The bride and groom were expected anytime after going to visit an ailing aunt in Seven Poplars.

"It was even more fun when the older folks went home," Atarah's sister, Tamar, piped up. "I loved the singing."

"We don't get to sing fast hymns very often back in Kentucky," Atarah explained. "Our bishop thinks they'll lead us astray." She rolled her eyes.

Atarah and Tamar were identical twins and dressed, acted and sounded alike. They had heavy Kentucky accents when they spoke English. Their accents were so thick that at first, Ginger had had a hard time understanding what they were saying. Introduced to them the previous day at the wedding, Ginger could tell the two apart only by the dark mole on Atarah's cheek. Ginger had taken to the sisters immediately and ended up sitting with them for dinner and supper after the wedding because Joe hadn't asked her.

That afternoon there was a mixed crowd at Mary's house, though it was mostly folks in their twenties. Some of the women there were married, some walking out with prospective husbands, and others, like Atarah and Tamar, hoping to find someone special.

Ginger listened as she took two containers of leftover stuffed eggs from the wedding supper and combined them into one. It bothered her that she didn't know which group she was in. Was she spoken for or not? She thought that she and Joe had an agreement, even if he hadn't come straight out and said so. During the week, he gave her a ride home from Eli's most nights, and on weekends, they attended the same frolics, and he always took her home afterward. He'd even tried to kiss her one night, though she'd set him straight on that matter pretty quickly. That meant they were courting, didn't it? But then he'd basically ignored her at the wedding yesterday. She was confused and a little disheartened. And her mother's disapproval nagged at her. What if her mother was right? What if Joe wasn't a good match for her?

"*Hymns* are going to lead you astray?" Ellie, a friend of the bride's from Seven Poplars, slapped the kitchen counter with her hand from her perch on a stool and laughed. Ellie was a little person who, like Ginger's brother Ethan, was a schoolteacher. Ginger had heard that summer that now that Ellie was married to the farrier, Jakob, she would be resigning from her position to focus on her duties as a wife. So far, however, Ellie was still teaching. Ellie was in her late twenties, about four feet tall and quite attractive, with her neat figure, blond hair and blue eyes. Ellie's freckled face was as fair as any young woman's in Kent County, and she was always smiling and laughing.

With so many in town for Caleb and Mary's wedding, a whole weekend of festivities had been planned. That night the men were going to play a couple of rounds of *eck balle*, then there would be a bonfire supper followed by singing. There were hot dogs and sausages to roast to go along with the leftover macaroni and potato salads and creamed celery, among other dishes. And Mary's mother had bought four boxes of graham crackers, four bags of marshmallows and dozens of chocolate bars so everyone could make s'mores for dessert. The following afternoon, weather permitting, they had plans to have a spaghetti supper. The best part of the evening would be that the men would cook the noodles to go with the sauce already made and then serve the women.

"I don't think it's the hymns the bishop has a problem with, it's how rowdy the boys get," Tamar told her sister.

"*Ne*," Atarah disagreed. "I think he heard—"

"That there *was clapping*," Tamar finished.

The twin sisters looked at each other and giggled, making Ginger smile. She and Bay were fraternal twins and were close, but these two girls almost seemed more like one person than two. They even completed each other's sentences.

"Nothing like a good ole Amish scandal," Ellie remarked, shaking her head with a smile as she covered a casserole of hot baked beans and ground hamburger with foil.

"I thought Kent County never had scandals," a young woman with inky black hair covered with a black prayer kapp said. Ginger couldn't remember her name.

"I don't know about that. I heard Mary's mother talking to her sister about that handsome one," Tamar said conspiratorially. She began cutting a pan of lemon bars into squares.

"Joe Verkler," Atarah put in with a giggle. "He's—"

"*Trouble*," her sister said.

The moment Joe's name was mentioned, Ginger stiffened. Her first impulse was to defend Joe, but her curiosity won her over, and she concentrated on moving the last of the creamy eggs into their container as she listened. She imagined this was about Joe's sneakers with the Swoosh, and possibly the expensive sunglasses.

Older folks could get themselves worked up about things like that. To them, even a fancy pair of black sneakers represented change in their way of life, and it was important to their faith that they remain separate from the world. That they never become dependent upon it. It was a constant issue in Hickory Grove, in most Amish communities, really. It had been the same way in upstate New York, where Ginger had grown up. The churches constantly had to reassess their *Ordung,* which was the guide to community standards and the doctrine that defined sin. Sometimes the changes were forced upon them due to the shift from farm to nonfarm employment for men, like the necessity of cell phones. Other times, it was the younger men and women who pushed for simple changes like what board games were acceptable to play. Many men and women Ginger's age believed a simple board game wouldn't cause a misstep in faith. They believed their elders needed to have more trust in them than that.

"*Ya,*" Atarah went on. "That one with his long hair and fancy—"

"Sneakers," Tamar finished for her again.

Several of the unmarried girls giggled, and Ginger pressed her lips together. Maybe Joe's hair was a little longer than most men wore theirs, but it wasn't as if it was as long as a woman's. In her opinion, anyone worried about Joe's sneakers was making a mountain out of a molehill.

"*Ach.* Sneakers does not a man make." Ellie climbed down off her stool and, using hot mitts, carried the casserole dish of beans to the kitchen table. The plan was to gather all of the food for supper and then have the men carry it out to the picnic tables that had already been taken out to the field where they would have the bonfire.

At Ellie's gentle scolding, the giggling girls went quiet, busying themselves with their food preparation.

"And a man's footwear does not a scandal make," Ellie advised. "'The Lord seeth not as man seeth, for man looketh on the outward appearance, but the Lord looketh on the heart.'"

"It's not his shoes," the girl Ginger didn't know said in a hushed tone. "It's his *flirting*." She whispered the last word. "He was talking up my sister yesterday at the wedding, and she's just seventeen. *Unfitting*, my *mam* says."

"I heard someone saw him buying beer," one of the Fisher girls whispered loudly. She pointed a mayonnaise-covered spoon, motioning with it to emphasize her words. "In one of those *liquor stores*."

Atarah leaned forward, her eyes wide. "But how would anyone know that unless *they* were in the store?"

Alcoholic beverages were not allowed to be consumed among the Old Order Amish. That said, it was not unheard of for young men, not yet baptized, to dabble in beer consumption and even cigarette smoking. While the church districts in Kent County did not recognize *rumspringa*, Ginger knew from her brother living in Lancaster County, Pennsylvania, that it was accepted there. That was no excuse for Joe. But it might not even be true. What was more disturbing to Ginger was the possibility that Joe had been flirting with this girl's sister. Ginger assumed she and Joe were dating exclusively.

"I don't know," Tamar said. "Maybe one of the elders—"

A door off the kitchen opened and the tread of heavy footsteps sounded. It was one of the men.

"*Hist*," Ellie warned. "No one likes a gossip, men looking for wives least of all."

Everyone in the kitchen went quiet, returning to their tasks.

"Wow, you all sure are quiet." Caleb, the groom, walked into the kitchen and halted, hands on his hips. "Fire's going. We've got some boys outside who are hungry enough to eat a pork shoulder on their own. Think we can get some of those hot dogs? Just to hold us over? Maybe eat a little something and get this *eck balle* game going before it starts to get dark?"

Atarah reached for the platter of hot dogs she'd been preparing, but Ginger spoke before the girl could. "I'll bring them out," she volunteered, turning to face Caleb and blocking his view of Atarah.

"Oh." Caleb shrugged. "Okay, well…" He gazed around the room. "Mary will be inside in a minute. She got waylaid in the driveway by one of the neighbors."

The moment Caleb walked out of the kitchen, Ginger slid the serving plate of hot dogs off the counter. "I'll carry these out. Best make another plate," she told Atarah, grabbing a big bag of rolls off the kitchen table as she went by. "You don't know the men in Kent County. They can eat a lot."

Before Atarah or any of the other girls offered to take the hot dogs outside themselves, Ginger headed for the back door. She threw her jacket on and hurried outside.

Sidestepping a little spotted dog at the bottom of the porch steps, Ginger walked quickly across the barnyard, the dog following. They went through an open gate into the field. She was halfway to the blazing bonfire when she spotted Joe standing near her brother Levi, who was busy cutting wood. Levi was chopping and stacking. Joe was talking to someone else.

As Ginger set the plate and bag of rolls down on the nearest picnic table, Joe moved, and she spotted who he was talking to. It was Annie Swartzentruber. Ginger knew her from Spence's Bazaar. Her family sold baked goods and the most amazing cinnamon rolls. The rolls, which were the size of a dessert plate, were always sold out on Fridays by 11:00 a.m., no matter how many they made.

Joe said something to Annie that made her giggle, and Ginger felt her face grow hot with annoyance. Was he flirting with her? He was! Without a second thought, Ginger marched over to where the two were standing between the pile of wood to be burned and the fire. The sound of Levi's ax striking wood reverberated in the cool afternoon air.

"Hello, Annie," Ginger said, her voice tight.

Annie met Ginger's gaze with surprise, then embarrassment. As if she'd been caught doing something she knew she shouldn't be. So Joe *had* been flirting with her.

"Ginger." Annie nodded without making eye contact this time. "Guess I best go see if anyone needs help in the kitchen."

Ginger folded her arms over her chest. "I'm sure they could use your help."

Levi took one look at his stepsister, hearing the tone of her voice, and his eyes widened. He turned back to the pile of wood, lifted the ax and let it fall on a piece of thick wood with a loud crack.

Joe looked at Levi, then back at Ginger. He gave her a big smile, and she felt herself melting inside. "I was just looking for you," he said.

She set her jaw. She wasn't going to let him get away with it this time. "No, you were not. You were flirting with Annie." She pointed in the direction the girl had just gone.

"Flirting?" He slid his hands into his pockets, making a face that suggested Ginger was mistaken. "I was just talking."

"Talking, my eye," she sputtered. "I heard her giggling!" She crossed her arms again and turned toward the blazing fire. There was a pile of small branches, and she picked one up to add to the fire.

Joe touched her arm and moved up beside her. "Ginger, I can't help it if she laughed. I don't even know her." He gestured in the direction Annie had gone. "I was just being polite."

Ginger eyed Joe, then turned to her stepbrother. "Levi, you think Joe was flirting with Annie?"

"Don't get me involved in this. I'm just chopping wood for the bonfire." Levi sank the ax into a log that was the size of a peck basket, grabbed several pieces of freshly cut wood and walked around to the other side of the bonfire.

It was on the tip of Ginger's tongue to straight-out ask Joe if they were walking out together or not, but then she suddenly grew worried that this was all her fault. What if she wasn't a good girlfriend? What if Joe was seeking out another girl's company because she was too boring or…or… Whatever.

Ginger moved closer to the bonfire and poked at it with the branch. The fire cracked and popped and sent sparks flying. One stung her on the back of her hand, and she flung the branch. "Ouch!" She looked at her hand, and by the bright light of the flames, she could see a red welt already bubbling up. "I burned myself," she said.

He stepped closer. "Ginger," he said sweetly. "I hope you're not upset about Annie. It was completely innocent."

She pressed the back of her hand to her mouth. It was already blistering up. She needed to get some salve for it and maybe a Band-Aid.

"I already told you, you're the girl for me." He gazed into her eyes with his big blue eyes. "So stop worrying your pretty head. Let's have some fun."

The way he was smiling at her, she couldn't help but smile back. He was right, of course. They *were* here to have fun. So she put on her sweetest smile and let him tell her about his *eck balle* strategy.

Chapter Five

"Don't worry."

It had sounded easy enough when Joe had said it, but the following morning, Ginger was still worrying. She kept going over in her head what she could do differently so Joe wouldn't want to flirt with other girls like Annie. She didn't know what to do to keep him interested in her. Because they were a good match. He'd said so himself. Everyone in Hickory Grove thought they looked like the perfect couple. Perfect for each other.

Well…except her mother. And her twin sister.

Ginger needed to talk to someone about Joe, but who? Her mother certainly wouldn't be receptive. Nor Bay. And her younger sisters wouldn't understand. While they were attending frolics now, neither had gotten serious with anyone yet. Ginger had thought about visiting her older sister, Lovey. She lived close enough to walk, but Lovey and Marshall's little one, Elijah, had taken sick with a bad cold the morning of the wedding, and Ginger didn't want to bother her.

Of course, Ginger did have a few girlfriends she

might be able to talk with, but lately, it was Eli who was her confidant. Not that they talked about Joe exactly, but Eli was always easy to talk to. And such a good listener. He seemed to know when she just wanted him to listen while she worked something out or when she wanted advice. When she talked, he gave her his full attention. And he managed to beat her at Chinese checkers at the same time.

The thought made her smile.

She wondered if Eli would be a good person to talk to about Joe. Eli was, after all, a man. Maybe he could offer some insight.

Ginger went through her weekend morning routine as she mulled over the situation. She washed her face, brushed her teeth, dressed in an everyday dress and apron and tied a scarf on her head. She made breakfast with her mother and sisters: scrambled eggs and scrapple, apple cinnamon muffins fresh out of the oven and buttered sourdough toast. After the morning meal, she did dishes and took the scraps out to the chickens. As she was coming back into the house, she ran into her mother. Actually bumped into her, because she wasn't paying attention to where she was going.

Her mother caught her by the shoulders and looked into Ginger's eyes, her own eyes twinkling with amusement. "Woolgathering, *Dochtah*?"

"*Ne*…" Ginger moved the scraps pail from one hand to the other. The back of her hand, covered by a Band-Aid, was still tender from where she had burned it the previous day. "*Ya*, I suppose I was."

Her mother narrowed her gaze, studying Ginger. "I recognize that look. A woman your age can't help but think about husbands and babies after attending a wedding."

Ginger felt herself blush, embarrassed by the mention of babies. Of course she wanted children, but she wasn't ready to think of Joe and babies in the same thought.

"Plenty of nice young men visiting Hickory Grove this weekend," her mother went on. She was wearing an everyday dress that was rose-colored. Her hair was covered with a blue scarf, and she wore her reading glasses dangling from a piece of ribbon around her neck. Though her stepson Joshua and his wife, Phoebe, would make her a grandmother again in the spring, she certainly didn't look old enough to be one. "And some *goot* choices living right here."

Ginger didn't say anything. She already knew her mother didn't approve of Joe. She wasn't going to remind her that she'd already made her choice. And that it was Ginger's choice to make.

Her mother was quiet for what seemed like a very long time. She just stood there in the mudroom, looking at Ginger, somehow making her feel unsettled. Then at last, her mother said, "What are your plans for the day? Are you joining the girls at Mary's house to see the wedding gifts?"

Caleb and Mary had opened their gifts at the wedding, but there had been so many that her mother had invited all of Mary's friends over for gingerbread and hot cocoa to see what she'd been given.

"*Ya,* I think I will, but that's not until two." She met her mother's gaze. She trusted Eli, and she knew nothing she said would go beyond the two of them.

"If you don't need me for anything, I was thinking I'd run over to Eli's."

"Oh?" Her mother raised her eyebrows.

Ginger's mother broke into a smile. "Eli's? On your day off? I see."

I see? What did that mean? There was something about her tone that concerned Ginger. "I… I want to take the children some of the apple muffins we made this morning." Not exactly a fib. She *had* thought that morning at breakfast that the little ones would enjoy the fresh muffins. And Lizzy had lost so much weight during her illness that her pediatrician had encouraged Eli to increase her food intake. "Eli is a pretty good cook, but his baking?" She shook her head.

"Taking muffins to the children?" her mother asked. "And you're not going for any other reason? *On your day off*," she added.

"What other reason would I have?" Ginger asked, confused by her mother's tone and demeanor. What did her *mam* know that Ginger didn't? She took a step to the side to go around her.

But her mother didn't budge. And she was still smiling.

"Is… Is it okay that I go?" Ginger asked. "I'm not scheduled to work at the harness shop today."

"Of course. I think Eli's children would love some apple muffins." Finally, she stepped aside to let her daughter pass. "And I imagine Eli would enjoy a muffin, as well."

It was clear now by her *mam*'s tone as to her meaning. That Eli *liked* her.

The idea of it scared Ginger. And intrigued her at the same time.

* * *

Ginger spent the entire ride over to Eli's on her push scooter thinking not about her problem with Joe, but about her mother's insinuation. It wasn't until the family dog greeted her at the end of the lane that she pushed aside thoughts of Eli, because it was a ridiculous idea. Eli didn't *like* her. Not *that* way. And she… She certainly didn't—well, it didn't matter what feelings she might or might not have for her employer because she already had a beau. And *that* was why she was coming to see Eli in the first place.

The dog barked and raced in a tight circle around Ginger's push scooter. "Careful!" she warned with a laugh. "You're going to—"

Suddenly, Molly cut so close in front of Ginger's scooter that she had to turn the front wheel sharply to avoid hitting the dog. As she did, she slid in some loose gravel. One second she was balanced on her push scooter, and the next, she was lying on her side, the scooter on top of her. "Ouch," she muttered, stunned momentarily. She lifted her head, then lowered it to the ground again to catch her breath.

Molly pushed her cold, wet nose against Ginger's face.

"Ew, no." She gave the dog a gentle push and then got to her feet. The backpack of muffins on her back was still there and she hadn't squished them. She carefully moved each arm and leg. She was fine, nothing broken. Her dress was dirty, but somehow wasn't torn. Her cheekbone stung and she pressed her fingertips to it. She winced. Just a scrape. The only real pain she had was at her elbow. It burned. She raised her arm to see a tear in her denim coat. She poked her fingers through the hole to her elbow and felt something wet and warm. Blood.

"Look what you've done," she told the dog, wiping her fingers on the front of the coat. The blood could be washed out, the coat patched. She looked at the dog as she picked up her scooter. "You could have been hurt if I'd hit you," she told it.

Molly just sat in the middle of the lane, looking up at her with big brown eyes. It was the dog's eyes that had gotten under Eli's skin when he'd found her in that parking lot. That was what he had told Ginger, and she completely understood. In many ways, Eli reminded her of her stepfather, Benjamin. Benjamin wore his heart on his sleeve, and he wasn't embarrassed by it. At first, it had taken some getting used to, seeing him show his affection for her mother. Ginger had never doubted her father had loved her mother or her and her siblings, but he'd not been a demonstrative man. He hadn't been one for words or physical affection; he had shown his love for his family in his deeds. This was refreshing, though. And she liked the trait in Eli.

Molly trotted up the driveway, then stopped and turned back as if waiting for Ginger.

"I'm coming," she told Molly. She shifted her backpack. At least the muffins hadn't been ruined. She lifted the scooter's handlebars and began to push it up the lane, deciding not to get on it again.

Phillip greeted them in the barnyard. "Ginger's here!" the five-year-old shouted. He dropped the handle of a red wagon he'd been pulling and ran toward her. "*Dat*! Ginger's here!"

When the boy started to run, the dog got excited and began to bark.

All thoughts of her little mishap went out the window at the sound of Phillip's excitement to see her.

"Ginger's here!" shouted Andrew, coming out of the granary with a bucket of ears of field corn.

A moment later, Simon appeared in the doorway of the granary. "Ginger!" His face lit up and her heart melted.

While Eli's oldest boy was the most reserved, he'd quickly taken to her. In the last weeks they had formed a special bond, so special that he had begun giving her a quick hug before she left each day, and he seemed to appreciate her affection for him. Unlike the other children, he remembered his mother well, and missed her all the more for it, Ginger thought. Not that she felt she was in any way replacing his mother, but she was willing to do anything she could to help Eli's children. She'd become so attached to them in the month since she'd begun watching them that she didn't want even to consider what would happen when Eli's job was done and he didn't need her anymore.

All three boys were dressed for outdoor chores in patched denim trousers with denim coats and a knit cap pulled down over their ears. They needed haircuts, she noticed. She'd have to say something to Eli. She'd be happy to cut their hair, but she didn't want to overstep her bounds.

"What are you doing here?" Simon set down the bucket and walked toward her.

"Did you come to play?" Phillip asked in Pennsylvania *Deitsch*. His cap was too big for him and was threatening to cover his eyes, but he didn't seem to notice. "Can I ride your scooter?" He grabbed the handlebars, which were almost as tall as he was. "*Dat* says when I go to school next year, I can have a scooter like Simon and Andrew." He made a face. "But he says I have to wear an orange vest so Englishers can see me." He frowned.

"He thinks school will be fun," Andrew told her, joining them. He rolled his eyes comically at Ginger.

Ginger chuckled, and then looked down at Phillip. She pushed his cap back so she could see his eyes again. "You *can* try my scooter but it's big for you," she said in English. "I think you'd do better trying one of your brothers'."

He gripped the handlebars, testing them out. "But yours is *blau* and theirs is *schwarz*."

"*Ya*, mine is blue. And theirs are black," she said, not directly correcting his speech. Though Phillip wasn't in school yet, Eli believed that he should be speaking English as well as his native tongue.

"Blue," he repeated, and grinned. "*Ya*. Yours is blue."

"Ginger!"

She turned around to see Lizzy running out of the barn, bundled in a coat, a knit cap on her head, a scarf around her neck and gloves on her hands. "I said you was coming!" she cried in Pennsylvania *Deitsch* as she raced across the yard as fast as her little legs could carry her. Her cheeks shone bright and rosy. "*Dat* said you weren't, but I knew you were." Reaching Ginger, the little girl threw her arms around Ginger's legs. She peered up, switching to English. "I *misshed* you."

Ginger laughed and squatted down to hug Lizzy. "And I missed you."

All talking at once, the three boys gathered around Ginger's scooter and rolled it away.

"I thought I heard your voice."

Ginger glanced up as Eli strode out of the barn, and the strangest sensation went through her. He looked the same as always and yet… Somehow, he seemed different. Why? How? Was it because her mother had suggested Eli liked her—the way a boy likes a girl? Lots of boys and men found her attractive. That didn't matter to her. What she looked like was God's doing, not her own.

She watched Eli as he walked toward her, seeing him in a different light than she had seen him before.

He liked her.

And if she was completely honest with herself, she *liked* him, too.

"What brings you here?" Eli was smiling. "Not that you have to have a reason to come by. You know you're always welcome. The children were disappointed this morning that it was a Saturday and you wouldn't be here. Lizzy wanted me to bring her to your house at about six, but I didn't know that you would appreciate such an early visit."

His laugh was easy and comforting in the way that a cozy blanket or a cup of hot chocolate was on a cold evening.

Ginger slowly came to her feet, looking up at him. "You could have brought her over. I was up."

Lizzy remained where she was, holding on to Ginger's apron.

"I brought the children some muffins," Ginger explained. "We made them fresh this morning. I don't know what Nettie was thinking but she made enough for everyone in Hickory Grove."

Eli looked down at his daughter. "Did you hear that, *boppli*?" He reached out and touched Lizzy's cheek, the smile suddenly disappearing from his face. "She seems warm. Does she seem warm to you?" He touched his daughter's face again and Lizzy wiggled away. "And her cheeks are red. Lizzy, are you feeling all right?" He frowned, pushing his knit cap back on his head. "I knew I shouldn't have brought her outside," he fretted. "It's nearly fifty degrees, but the wind—"

"Eli, she's fine," Ginger assured him with a laugh. "She just looks overheated. Which is no wonder. You've just got her wrapped up too much. Are you hot, my Lizzy?" She unwound the scarf from the little girl and removed it and then unbuttoned the top button of her coat that was a soft navy corduroy. "Better?"

Lizzy bobbed her head.

Ginger removed the knit cap from Lizzy's head for good measure and straightened her headscarf. "You worry too much, Eli. She's fine," she repeated, this time softly.

He closed his eyes for a moment, then opened them. "You're right. I know you are." He opened his arms, then let them fall to his sides. "Claudia says I need to stop fussing over her. It's just that she was so sick, and I was so—" He frowned and narrowed his gaze. "Ginger, what happened to you?" His face became a mask of concern, now for her. He reached out to touch her cheek.

She ducked to avoid his hand. "I'm fine. I fell in the lane." She grinned at him, feeling silly, though not embarrassed. Everyone took a spill on their push scooter once in a while. Two weeks ago, one of the men who worked for her stepfather at the harness shop, while on his scooter, had to move over to give a pickup truck as much room as possible. He'd slid off the pavement into a ditch and broken a finger in the tumble. Ginger hadn't broken anything. Besides, she and Eli were friends. There was no need to be embarrassed with a good friend.

And he *was* a good friend. She knew that because the moment she had arrived, she'd felt as if the burden on her shoulders had lightened. Joe's flirtation with Annie at the bonfire the previous day seemed less important being here with Eli. And the children. The children, who lived each day without their mother and still managed to laugh and hide cookies, reminded her to keep her troubles with her beau in perspective. God truly was good.

"Let me see," Eli insisted, taking her arm and gently turning her so she faced him.

Ginger winced as he bent her arm at the elbow.

He turned her arm to get a look at the tear in her coat. "Do you think it needs an X-ray?" His face was lined with concern, his blue eyes piercing. "I have a cell phone for emergencies. We can call a driver."

"*Ne*, I'm fine." She pulled away, wincing again as she straightened her arm. It was already beginning to swell.

"You're *not* fine. You're bleeding and it looks like there's swelling." He glanced down at Lizzy, who was looking up at him. The red circles on her cheeks had faded. "Let's take Ginger inside and fix her boo-boo," he said.

"Eli…" Ginger rolled her eyes.

"Would you like to help your *dadi*?" Eli asked his daughter, ignoring Ginger.

The little girl bobbed her head up and down. "I'll be the *peedy-tishun*," she said.

Ginger chuckled. "The what?"

"Pediatrician," Eli translated.

"Ah." Ginger nodded. "Good word, Lizzy."

"Boys, I want you to finish your chores," Eli called to his sons. As he spoke, he eased the backpack off Ginger's back and slung it over his shoulder. "And no fighting," he warned. "Or it will be slug stew and spider biscuits for supper tonight."

Lizzy giggled as she set off for the house, leading the way. "No *shlug shtew, Dat*. I don't like to eat *shlugs*."

"Come on. Inside with you." Eli gently prodded Ginger forward.

"Eli, I'm fine," she argued, though she was already walking to the house.

"You're not," he said. Then he stopped and looked into her eyes. "You do so much for me, Ginger," he said quietly. "Let me do this for you."

He held her gaze for a long moment and she thought about the night before when she burned the back of her hand. Joe hadn't even acknowledged the injury. Joe, who was supposed to be her sweetheart. It didn't even hurt today, but that didn't matter. What mattered was that Joe hadn't cared all that much about her well-being.

And Eli did.

Chapter Six

In the gray light of early dawn, Ginger crept from the bed she shared with Bay and hurriedly dressed. It was a church Sunday, and they would be attending service at the Grubers' house midmorning. Ginger would change into her Sunday dress after breakfast, but for now, she dressed comfortably, throwing an old knit shawl over her shoulders.

It was going to be another cold day. The wind had been bitter the evening before when she and her sisters had returned home from the frolic at Mary's parents' place. They'd had a grand time there, though, looking through Mary's wedding gifts while sharing hot chocolate and cakes and cookies.

As she dressed, Ginger could hear the wind outside their window and wondered if there would be snow flurries.

The house was quiet. Usually, even at this hour, her *mam* was bustling around downstairs, one of her sisters was snoring and someone was banging on her little brother Jesse's door, calling him to get up for milking.

When Ginger went to her bedroom window and pulled back the curtain, she understood the silence that seemed to blanket the house. The ground was covered with snow, and large flakes were coming down so thickly that she could barely make out the roofline of the *gross-dadi* house in the orchard.

Her oldest stepbrother, Ethan, had been building it, intending to bring his new bride, Abigail, and her son there after his marriage. But Abigail's mother had dementia, and Ethan decided it was best to move in with Abigail rather than bring his bride home. When he'd decided *not* to live on the family farm, Ginger had been so proud of him. His love for Abigail was stronger than his pull to tradition, and that had made her love him all the more for it.

For now, the small *grossdadi* house stood empty. *Watching the family*, Ginger thought. Waiting to see who would take residence. At some point, Benjamin and her mother would move into the house, once their adult children were married and gone. But with Ethan now settled down the road with his new wife, who would eventually take the big house was unknown.

Ginger squinted, looking out the window, and then smiled. Snow...

Delaware rarely saw snowfalls of more than just a dusting, and certainly not before Christmas, but the fall had been colder than usual. Eli had told her the previous day that the *Farmer's Almanac* was predicting a hard winter with several big snowstorms. He'd wondered aloud if it was due to climate change, something the farmers talked a lot about. She'd asked how often the almanac was correct in its predictions. He'd told her it was right often enough to make him move his potted herbs closer to the house and wrap them in burlap to protect them. That was when he told her the herbs had been his wife's. Then he'd apologized for bringing her up so often. Ginger had told him that she didn't mind. What she didn't say was that she liked him all the more for the fact that, though his wife was gone, he hadn't forgotten her.

Ginger padded down the hall to the bathroom in her stocking feet. Although she loved her big blended family dearly, it was nice to not have to wait to brush her teeth or get into the shower. And it was better yet to be able to think about everything that had happened the previous day and remember all the details of her visit with Eli, uninterrupted.

Ginger had gone to Eli's with the intention of asking his thoughts on Joe, hoping to get some insight. But she had soon realized she didn't want to talk to him about Joe.

Sitting in Eli's kitchen while he made up a pan of hot soapy water for her to wash her wound, she'd recognized that the real reason she had come to Eli's was to be with him. And with the children. She had wanted to talk to him, not Joe. She had wanted to hear about the mantelpiece Eli was building for Verkler Construction's client. She had wanted to hear about how his old mare Bess's leg was coming along. After cutting it on a bit of tin roof that had blown off the corncrib, Eli had been concerned the wound wasn't healing. And that he might have to put her down. But the Amish veterinarian from Seven Poplars had come the evening before, cleaned the wound and given the mare an antibiotic.

She wasn't out of the woods yet, but Eli was hopeful she would come around.

Eli had fussed over Ginger's little accident as if she had been involved in a car crash on the highway. At first, his attention had flustered her. But it had also made her feel cared for. Since then, she hadn't been able to stop comparing Joe and Eli. Friday night, Joe hadn't even acknowledged the burn on her hand. Eli, on the other hand, had treated her banged-up elbow as if it was a major injury. He had cared for her wound and treated her with such gentle kindness. Her visit to Eli's had turned out to be a wonderful morning that slipped carelessly into afternoon.

They had made a beef stew together. It had started out with him asking her how to brown the meat, and what vegetables to put in. Then it had turned into her showing him how to make it, which had turned into him pitching in. He'd peeled potatoes and cut up onions, and he'd even run outside and taken a clipping of the last of his thyme from a pot of herbs he'd moved to the south side of the house to protect it from the weather. The thyme had been his idea. It wasn't an herb her *mam* put in her stew, but Eli had been right when he'd suggested it might work in the recipe. The subtle taste had been amazing.

It had intrigued her that Eli was interested in cooking, then tickled her when she saw how easily he took to it. She'd never known an Amish man who cooked. And after they'd made the stew, she had whipped up caramel sauce with brown sugar, vanilla and canned milk. She and Eli and the children had all sat around the table eating apple slices with the warm, sticky caramel.

When Lizzy had grown fatigued, Eli had sent his boys out to play, built a fire in the fireplace in their living room and laid Lizzy down on the couch with her doll. Eli and Ginger had then sat down at a small table to play Chinese checkers while they kept Lizzy company. The little girl was soon asleep, and Eli and Ginger had chatted as they played. They talked about all sorts of things, some not so serious, like what kind of pie was their favorite. They both loved sweet potato. Other conversations were more serious, like the changes that ought to be made to the *Ordung* in their church district.

Ginger had felt as if she had only been at Eli's a short time, but suddenly, it had been half past one. She'd ended up being late to Mary's because she had to go home and hook up the buggy so she and her sisters could go together.

Finishing up in the bathroom, Ginger went downstairs to build up the fire in the woodstove. They didn't need the woodstove to heat the house. Benjamin had added propane heat to the place when he bought it. But her *mam* loved making stews and soups on it and loved the way it made the kitchen cozy on cold mornings. There would be no cooking that day because it was the Sabbath, so starting the woodstove would allow the family to have a hot breakfast rather than a cold one. The day before, her youngest sister, Tarragon, whom they called Tara, had baked two huge egg, cheese and sausage casseroles, which would reheat well in the woodstove's oven.

Once the fire was going, Ginger went to the refrigerator to remove the breakfast casseroles. To do so, she had to step over the two Chesapeake Bay retrievers sleeping sprawled out in the middle of the kitchen floor. Her stepbrother Jacob wasn't supposed to let the dogs in the house at night. Her mother didn't like animals in the house because they made such a mess. But Silas and Ada often found their way into the house at night, especially when it was cold out, and her *mam* never did anything more than fuss about them after the fact.

Ada waggled her tail as Ginger took care not to step on her. Silas never moved.

Once the casseroles were in the woodstove oven and the fire had been stoked, Ginger stood in the kitchen listening to the quiet. Even on a Sunday, there were things to be done. The whole family would be awake soon. She already heard stirrings, and she wasn't quite ready to immerse herself in the controlled chaos of a Sabbath morning. Her youngest brothers, the twins born to her mother and Benjamin, would be demanding breakfast at once and have to be appeased with coffee mugs of dry cereal while the casserole reheated. Her sisters would fill the kitchen with breakfast preparations and gossip about what had gone on the night before at Mary's house. Her little brother Jesse would come downstairs begging for someone to help him find his Sunday-best clothes before he went to the barn. And her stepbrothers would fill up the kitchen and mudroom with their big bodies and bigger voices.

On impulse, Ginger went into the mudroom, took one of the many denim barn coats off a hook and put it on.

"Come along," she called to the two dogs as she tied a wool scarf over her head. Ada and Silas jumped to their feet and raced for the door Ginger held open for them.

With the dogs outside before her mother came down to her kitchen, Ginger would be sparing everyone in the family her fussing.

Outside, Ginger walked through the inch or two of snow, falling flakes hitting her on the cheeks. She looked up into the sky and wondered if the sun would come out later. It would be a pretty buggy ride to church service if it did.

Inside the barn, Ginger went where their cows were stalled. Normally it was the boys' chore to milk. Ginger hadn't had to milk a cow since her mother married Benjamin more than three years ago. Most of the time, she was thankful for that, but sometimes she became nostalgic, remembering what it had been like before her mother remarried. After their father had died, they had all been so sad, but their grief had united her sisters and their mother. The pettiness teenage girls could find so easily fell away, and they had worked together to keep the farm going. And with only a little brother not old enough to be much help, Ginger and her sisters had taken up many outside chores. One of Ginger's jobs had been milking. There was something about a cold winter morning and the warmth of a barn that always made her heart sing.

"Time for milking," she announced as a white cat rubbed against her leg, purring loudly.

Two of their cows would be calving in the spring and had about gone dry. Their young Guernsey, Petunia, however, still had plenty of milk to give. She'd had a late calf and was still producing well.

"Good girl," Ginger crooned to the fawn-and-white cow with the large brown eyes. "Nice girl. Nice, Petunia." She washed the cow's udder with warm soapy water that she got from the tap. Then she poured a measure of feed into the cow's trough and settled onto a milking stool. As she rested her head against Petunia's side and streams of milk poured into the shiny stainless steel bucket, her heart swelled with joy as she thought of all the gifts the Lord had bestowed on her rather than mulling over her problems with Joe.

She had a wonderful mother and siblings, stepfather and stepbrothers, a home that she loved and the security of the faith and community that surrounded her. She needed to stop obsessing over Joe. She had assumed God had put him in her path so she could marry him, but what if she was wrong? After all, Eli had been in Byler's that day, as well. Had God meant Eli for her all along, and had she just not seen it? She was confused about her feelings. Was Eli the man for her?

Or what if God didn't intend for her to marry either of them?

It was the Sabbath, a day to remind herself that no human could hope to understand God's ways, least of all her. What she *could* do was work each day to appreciate the bounty He had blessed her with. With that thought, she closed her eyes.

As she prayed, the level of the milk rose in the pail, smelling sweet and fresh. Among other things, she prayed for God to heal Eli's sorrow from when he had spoken of the thyme and his wife. She also prayed for patience for herself, patience to wait to hear God's will. To listen for it and not confuse her human wants with God's plan.

Ginger finished, as always, with the Lord's Prayer

and a plea that God guide her mind, hands and footsteps through the day to help her serve her family and faith according to His intentions. She was about to murmur a devout "amen" when one last prayer slipped between her lips. "And please, God, could you show me the way to a husband?"

"Smells delicious, Claudia," Eli said as he walked into his sister's kitchen in his stocking feet. Every time he came into her house, she told him he needn't take his boots off, but it was a habit he couldn't break. Lizzy's shoes were in the mudroom, as well. And his boys' boots would be there as soon as they came into the house with their cousins. It just seemed like the polite thing to do—not to track dirt into his sister's clean house. The only downside was that everyone could see your socks, know if they were clean or mismatched. Today he was wearing a sock with a hole in it. He'd learned many domestic skills since his wife died, but darning wasn't one of them.

Claudia stood at the stove, her back to him. She was stirring a pot, and the whole room smelled of sauerkraut with roast pork and dumplings. Biscuits, too. When Eli and Claudia were children, their mother always served the main meal of the day at one o'clock in the afternoon and supper was cold sandwiches or leftovers from the midday meal. However, like most Amish families, Claudia's husband, John, worked off the farm during the week; he was a mason by trade. So Claudia served the biggest meal of the day in the evening when the family could gather together as one.

"New hot water heater is all hooked up," Eli told his sister.

Her husband, John, had purchased a new water heater when their old one had sprung a leak. Eli had experience installing a new propane gas hot water heater because he'd done so in his own home. "Two are better than one; because they have a good reward for their labour." That had always been one of his grandmother's favorite Bible verses.

Eli walked to the kitchen counter where a tray of biscuits was cooling and pinched a piece off one. He popped it in his mouth. It was crisp and soft and buttery all at the same time. "John is just breaking down the cardboard shipping box," he told his sister. "Said to tell you he'll be up shortly for supper."

Claudia turned around and he noticed that she was wearing a clean apron and had replaced her head scarf with a white prayer *kapp*. She was looking rather formal for a weekday supper at home. "Eli, I want you to meet Elsie." She indicated the large kitchen table behind him. "Elsie Swartzentruber." She smiled sweetly at him. "Remember, I was telling you about her?"

Startled to realize someone else was in the room, Eli turned to see a petite woman sitting at the table filling a salt shaker. She was attractive, with dark eyes and a dimpled chin. For a moment, he didn't say anything. He was annoyed that his sister had invited Elsie to supper on the same night she had invited him and his children. This was obviously a setup.

But that wasn't Elsie's fault.

He smiled and nodded. "*Guter owed*, Elsie." He suddenly felt self-conscious about the hole in his sock.

"Elsie's son, Abner, is the same age as Andrew," Claudia said. "They're here visiting from Ohio."

He cut his eyes at his sister, then looked back to Elsie, who had slid to the edge of her seat, obviously eager to meet him.

"Elsie, do you mind if I borrow my sister for a second?"

"*Ne*," Elsie murmured.

Eli pointed to the hallway that led to a living room large enough to host church for their district. Though they only lived two miles away, Claudia and John belonged to a different church district than Eli.

With an impatient sigh, Claudia followed him down the hall.

In the living room, Lizzy was playing on the floor near the woodstove with her two cousins, Mary John and Anne. The little girls were busy dressing clothespin dolls with scraps of fabric and paid the adults no mind.

Eli rested his hands on his hips. As he spoke, he tried to remind himself that Claudia only had his best interest at heart. "You invited Elsie to dinner without telling me?"

"Would you have come if I had?"

"*Ne*."

She shrugged. "So there you have it."

"There I have *what*?" Eli let out his breath. "The children and I are going home. I won't be put in this position, and you shouldn't have put Elsie in it, either. I told you I wasn't interested in you setting me up on a date."

"It's not a date," she argued. "It's supper. On a weeknight," she added as if that made all the difference.

"But you were hoping I'd find Elsie agreeable and

then ask her on a date." He pointed in the direction of the kitchen, trying to keep his voice down. "And *she* thinks that's why she's here. Why *I'm* here."

Claudia shook her finger at him as if he was a boy again and not widowed with four children. "Eli, if you're going to be contrary, she's not going to want to go anywhere with you."

He threw up his hands. "I don't want to go on a date with her!"

The girls all looked up at him, and he turned his back to them, lowering his voice. "I told you," he whispered harshly, "when you mentioned Elsie before, that I wasn't interested."

She crossed her arms. "Because of Ginger Stutzman?" she said. "Because you think she's going to fall in love with you, and you're going to marry her."

He hesitated. A few days ago, he might have disagreed, but after Ginger's visit Saturday, when she'd shown up unexpectedly... Somehow the impossible didn't seem quite so impossible anymore. Something had changed between him and Ginger, though he didn't know how or exactly when. But what he did know was that there was an attraction between them that he hadn't felt before.

And things weren't going well with Ginger and Joe. It wasn't much of a courtship, and he sensed Ginger was beginning to realize that now. She hadn't come right out and said so, but he could tell something was different in her. In how she looked at Joe. But more importantly, in how she looked at him.

After Ginger's tumble on her scooter, Eli had taken her inside and cleaned up the scrape on her elbow and put ice on it to keep down the swelling. He suspected she'd come for some reason other than to deliver the muffins. She could have brought them easily enough on Monday. Instead, she had come on a Saturday morning when she didn't have to be there for work. He guessed she had wanted to talk to him about something, maybe even about Joe, but she'd never brought him up. That was fine with him, because he'd have had to be forthright with her and tell her exactly what he thought.

She'd ended up staying for hours, which had delighted the children. And him. They'd ended up making beef stew together. It was still a fairly new experience for him because he'd never cooked with someone else before Ginger. His wife had always done the cooking, and after she had passed, either he cooked alone or was at the mercy of his sister or neighbors to provide meals.

Moving around the kitchen with Ginger had been so easy, so comfortable. Just thinking about it made him smile. He'd had a whole list of chores to do, plus he'd intended to repair a blade on his windmill. Instead, he'd whiled away hours with Ginger, talking and playing games like he had in his younger days back when he was single and courting girls.

It was while they were chatting and playing Chinese checkers that Eli had realized she was looking at him differently than before. There was something in her voice, a tenderness, and a sparkle in her eyes he hadn't seen. That was when it occurred to him that there just might be a spark of attraction there. That maybe it wasn't one-sided anymore.

Just thinking about their day together made his heart swell. Ginger had stayed so long that she'd been late going home to pick up her sisters to visit with Mary, the new bride.

"Eli."

The tone of Claudia's voice pulled him from his thoughts. His sister had said something to him that he had missed. He waited, hoping she would repeat the question and not realize he hadn't been listening.

"Is that what you honestly think?" she asked, obviously as annoyed with him as he was with her. "Because if you do, you're a fool. Girls like Ginger don't marry men like you, men nearly ten years older. With four children," she added pointedly.

Eli stood there for a moment, wiggling his big toe that poked out from his sock. "Claudia," he said quietly. "I can't help how I feel."

She sighed again, but this time it was a kinder sigh. Gentler. "I know you can't, little brother. I'm just trying to protect you from a broken heart."

He mulled that over for a moment. "I know you're probably right," he said finally. "But wouldn't it be worth a try? Just in case Ginger is the woman for me? You know, I never thought I had a chance with Elizabeth, either. She was too smart, too beautiful." He met Claudia's gaze. "But she came to love me. And look at what a wonderful life we had together, even if it was too short. And had I not taken the chance, I wouldn't have our children now."

Claudia reached out and rubbed Eli's arm. "Will you at least come back and join us for supper?"

He smiled. "Of course, I will."

"And will you promise not to get your hopes up?" she asked. "About Ginger?"

"'Hope does not put us to shame because God has poured love into our hearts,'" he paraphrased from Romans. Then he walked down the hall to talk with Elsie. And tried not to think about the fact that it was Ginger he wished was joining them for supper instead.

Chapter Seven

Ginger sat on Eli's porch steps huddled in her cloak, trying not to be angry. It was well past dark, and still, Joe hadn't shown up. Eli had been out twice: first to tell her she should wait inside and the second time to offer to drive her home. She'd been stubborn and insisted on staying put on the porch.

Now Joe was nearly two hours late. He wasn't coming. Ginger knew that. She knew Eli knew.

Slowly she stood, wrapping her wool cloak around her. Her nose was cold and numb. So were her fingers because she had forgotten her gloves that morning. She sighed, thinking it was time to either start walking home or agree to let Eli take her home. She hated to do that but—

The sound of hoofbeats and buggy wheels sounded at the end of the lane, and she looked up. It was Joe. He hadn't forgotten her. He'd just been running late again. He did so much for his uncle these days, it was a wonder he ever left home on time, she told herself, trying to lift her spirits. Trying to convince herself she didn't know what she secretly knew: that Joe was no longer interested in her. That there were too many pretty new girls around with wedding guests still in town. Pretty girls who were younger than she was.

Ginger went down the steps to get a closer look. The snow from the weekend had melted into puddles and had been freezing at night, then thawing during the day, turning all the barnyards in the county into mud mires.

She lifted on her toes to get a glimpse of Joe's buggy. The lights on the front of the buggy looked familiar, but she didn't think they were Joe's. It was required by law that all buggies have a triangular slow-moving vehicle sign and lights, but there was no standard light configuration, so all of the buggies were slightly different.

She squinted, trying to see through the dark. The buggy coming up the lane didn't sound like Joe's two-seater, either. It sounded heavier.

Ginger spotted her stepfather's new driving horse trotting up the lane. For a moment, she tried to convince herself she was mistaken, but the gelding's high-stepping gait was unique. Then she recognized the old buggy her mother had brought with her into her second marriage, and her shoulders sagged. *That* was why the lights looked familiar.

The buggy entered the barnyard and circled, coming to a stop in front of Eli's porch. The driver's door slid open. It was Bay.

"What are you doing here?" Ginger asked dismally.

"Come to pick you up," her twin responded. "*Mam* sent me."

Ginger glanced back at the house as she circled the gelding. She spotted a curtain pulled back in the mudroom. She assumed it was one of the children, but it was Eli. He dropped the curtain when he saw her looking back at him.

Ginger opened the buggy door and climbed up and inside. "How did *Mam* know I needed a ride? Did Joe call the harness shop?"

Bay looked at her sternly, the dim interior light emphasizing the knit of her brows. "*Mam* said this late, he wasn't coming for you. The plan is for one of the boys to come for you if Joe doesn't show up, but—"

"Wait," Ginger said. "*Mam* has a plan for if Joe doesn't come for me?"

"Of course she does. She's still our mother. It doesn't matter how old we are. Anyway, one of the boys was supposed to fetch you, but they were all busy down at the barn fixing a gate. One of the hogs broke his way out and was headed down the middle of the road toward Lovey's place. Marshall spotted him. *Mam* was going to come herself but decided you'd be less cross with me."

"I wouldn't be cross with *Mam*," Ginger argued.

Bay gave her sister a look that meant she didn't believe her for a minute. "She watches the clock every weeknight, Ginger." She turned off the interior light, lifted the reins and urged the gelding forward. "Waiting for you to get home. Worrying over you."

Ginger sat back in the seat and pulled a wool blanket onto her lap. "She never told me that."

"I think she's trying not to interfere." Bay halted at the end of the driveway and waited for a little red car to pass before she pulled onto the road. "I think she's afraid if she says much, she'll drive the two of you closer."

Ginger looked at Bay, not angry, but upset with their mother. "How old does she think I am? I'm not a teen-age girl turning my head to every boy who smiles at me." She folded her arms over her chest. "Is that what *Mam* thinks?"

"I think she thinks you're headstrong. That you set your eye on Joe Verkler, and now you're determined not to change your mind about him. Even if he gives you reason," she said more gently.

Ginger stared out into the darkness. Her mother knew her too well. A pickup passed them, splashing water on the windshield. Bay turned on the wipers, and they rode half a mile without speaking. The inside of the buggy smelled of Bay's muddy boots and a sachet of herbs their mother kept under the dash.

"How was your day?" Ginger asked her sister, chang-ing the subject entirely.

"It was good. You wouldn't believe the number of orders coming into the greenhouse, not just for wreaths but swags and table arrangements, too. I don't know how we're going to fill them all. We're going to have to find another supplier for fresh greenery. I can't pick it all from our property. The place would be bald." She chuckled.

At first, Bay and their stepbrother Joshua's green-house that they had built the spring before had just been to sell plants in the spring and summer, maybe some gardening supplies. But when Bay had started making fresh wreaths, the business had taken off. They had got-ten so busy so quickly that Joshua's new wife, Phoebe, was helping out. And Bay was hiring a couple of young folks from their youth group to work Saturdays.

Bay looked at Ginger, "And now we have so many people signed up for the wreath-making class, Phoebe thinks we should offer a second session."

"*Ya*, I told Eli about making the wreaths. How you wanted to make it a family event. We thought we'd bring the children."

"*We?*" her sister asked. The controls on the dashboard dimly lit her face. English folks didn't realize it, but a buggy had a dashboard just like a car. From there, a driver controlled the lights, the windshield wipers and even a little heater sometimes.

"*Ya*, Eli and I. We thought we'd make a big wreath for the back door. Lizzy's probably young to do much, but the boys would enjoy it. And if there's cookies, hot chocolate and spiced cider being served, I imagine they'll love it. Eli said when he was growing up, they didn't do family projects like making Christmas decorations. I think because his mother died when he was young."

Bay looked at her funny.

"What?" Ginger asked.

For a moment her sister didn't say anything. There was just the sound of the gelding's rhythmic hoofbeats and the wooden wheels rolling on the pavement. A lot of Amish had rubber wheels now, but in Hickory Grove, they were still the traditional wood. Ginger had ridden in a rubber-wheeled buggy that summer while visiting friends in Lancaster County. She preferred the sound of the wooden wheels.

"What?" Ginger repeated. "Why are you looking at me like that, *Schweschder*?"

Bay had a silly little smile on her face, like a cat

caught lapping cream from a milk bucket. "You talk a lot about Eli."

"I spend a lot of time with him," Ginger responded, feeling as if she had to defend herself, though why she didn't know.

"Right. More time than you do with Joe," Bay observed. "And you talk about the children as if they're yours."

"I do not." Ginger turned on the leather bench seat to face her sister. "It's just that I'm with them all day and—" She went quiet.

Bay was right. She *did* talk about Eli's children as if they were hers. But wasn't that natural with how much time she spent with them? And them not having a mother?

Ginger thought before she spoke. "It's a lot for Eli to do alone. To take them places. I figured if we took them together, especially it being a Friday night, it would be easier. We could all go together after Eli gets home from work, and I wouldn't have to worry about Joe—" She fell into silence. The plan was a good one because these days, she couldn't rely on Joe to give her a ride home, could she?

"You know he's in love with you."

"Joe?" Ginger asked, frowning.

Bay laughed. "Don't be a silly goose. Joe doesn't love anyone but himself. I'm talking about *Eli*."

Ginger stared at her sister for a moment, glad she had leaned back on the seat so her face was in shadows. "He isn't," she heard herself say. But it came out as more of a question than an adamant denial.

"You know what I think?" Bay said. She went on

Get Up To 4 Free Books!

Dear Reader,

IT'S A FACT: if you answer 4 quick questions, we'll send you 4 FREE REWARDS from each series you try!

Try **Love Inspired® Romance Larger-Print** books and fall in love with inspirational romances that take you on an uplifting journey of faith, forgiveness and hope.

Try **Love Inspired® Suspense Larger-Print** books where courage and optimism unite in stories of faith and love in the face of danger.

Or **TRY BOTH!**

I'm not kidding you. As a leading publisher of women's fiction, we value your opinions... and your time. That's why we are prepared to reward you handsomely for completing our mini-survey. In fact, we have 4 Free Rewards for you, including 2 free books and 2 free gifts from each series you try!

Thank you for participating in our survey,

Pam Powers

To get your 4 FREE REWARDS:
Complete the survey below and return the insert today to receive up to 4 FREE BOOKS and FREE GIFTS guaranteed!

"4 for 4" MINI-SURVEY

1 Is reading one of your favorite hobbies?

☐ YES ☐ NO

2 Do you prefer to read instead of watch TV?

☐ YES ☐ NO

3 Do you read newspapers and magazines?

☐ YES ☐ NO

4 Do you enjoy trying new book series with FREE BOOKS?

☐ YES ☐ NO

Please send me my Free Rewards, consisting of **2 Free Books from each series I select** and **Free Mystery Gifts**. I understand that I am under no obligation to buy anything, as explained on the back of this card.

☐ **Love Inspired® Romance Larger-Print** (122/322 IDL GQ5X)
☐ **Love Inspired® Suspense Larger-Print** (107/307 IDL GQ5X)
☐ **Try Both** (122/322 & 107/307 IDL GQ6A)

FIRST NAME	LAST NAME

ADDRESS

APT.#	CITY

STATE/PROV.	ZIP/POSTAL CODE

EMAIL ☐ Please check this box if you would like to receive newsletters and promotional emails from Harlequin Enterprises ULC and its affiliates. You can unsubscribe anytime.

LI/SLI-520-MS20

HARLEQUIN READER SERVICE—Here's how it works:

Accepting your 2 free books and 2 free gifts (gifts valued at approximately $10.00 retail) places you under no obligation to buy anything. You may keep the books and gifts and return the shipping statement marked "cancel." If you do not cancel, approximately one month later we'll send you 6 more books from each series you have chosen, and bill you at our low, subscribers-only discount price. Love Inspired® Romance Larger-Print books and Love Inspired® Suspense Larger-Print books consist of 6 books each month and cost just $5.99 each in the U.S. or $6.24 each in Canada. That is a savings of at least 17% off the cover price. It's quite a bargain! Shipping and handling is just 50¢ per book in the U.S. and $1.25 per book in Canada*. You may return any shipment at our expense and cancel at any time — or you may continue to receive monthly shipments at our low, subscribers-only discount price plus shipping and handling. *Terms and prices subject to change without notice. Prices do not include sales taxes which will be charged (if applicable) based on your state or country of residence. Canadian residents will be charged applicable taxes. Offer not valid in Quebec. Books received may not be as shown. All orders subject to approval. Credit or debit balances in a customer's account(s) may be offset by any other outstanding balance owed by or to the customer. Please allow 3 to 4 weeks for delivery. Offer available while quantities last.

▲ If offer card is missing write to: Harlequin Reader Service, P.O. Box 1341, Buffalo, NY 14240-8531 or visit www.ReaderService.com ▲

BUSINESS REPLY MAIL
FIRST-CLASS MAIL   PERMIT NO. 717   BUFFALO, NY

POSTAGE WILL BE PAID BY ADDRESSEE

HARLEQUIN READER SERVICE
PO BOX 1341
BUFFALO NY 14240-8571

NO POSTAGE
NECESSARY
IF MAILED
IN THE
UNITED STATES

without waiting for Ginger to say she was interested in her sister's opinion. Big families were like that, always ready with an opinion whether you wanted it or not. "I think if you weren't so stubborn, if you weren't so obsessed with Joe Verkler, you'd admit that, while maybe you're not in love with Eli, you're sweet on him."

"I am not—" Ginger went quiet again, crossing her arms over her chest. Leaving the door open for her sister to go on. Because even though a part of her wanted to deny it, a part of her wanted to hear what her sister had to say. Was Eli really in love with her? Could that be possible? And if it was, how did she feel about it?

"*Mam* thinks Eli is more suitable for you than Joe, and so do I," Bay went on.

"Eli?" Ginger laughed. "We've known Eli for years now."

"What does that have to do with anything?" Bay asked.

Ginger couldn't come up with a snappy answer. Instead, she stared out the window. So what if she was a little sweet on Eli? How could any young woman who knew him not be? Unmarried women were attracted to unmarried men. It was part of God's plan. That didn't mean she wanted to marry Eli.

Did it?

Ginger stood in the hallway of John and Edna Fisher's house, her arms hanging at her sides, trying not to cry. Joe had said his piece and now had gone silent.

The house was filled with friends and neighbors, all gathered to celebrate Bishop Simon's fiftieth birthday. It had been a surprise supper party his wife, Annie, had cleverly planned for weeks. When the bishop arrived at the Fishers', he hadn't been the least suspicious of all the buggies in the barnyard because he thought he was there for a birthday party for John Fisher. John had been in on the whole thing, as had everyone from their church district. It was only when Bishop Simon walked into the house, carrying a dish of his wife's *boova shenkel*, and everyone hollered "Surprise!" that the ruse was up.

A potluck buffet supper had then been served, and now all of the dishes were being *ret* up in anticipation of an entire table of desserts, including a big chocolate cake with pink frosting, decorated with maraschino cherries.

"Joe," Ginger said softly, looking up at him. "Can we talk about this? *Please?*"

He stared at the polished wood floor for a long moment. The rooms around them were filled with people laughing and talking, babies crying, children squealing. There was joy all around Ginger. But none in her.

"I don't see the point," Joe muttered. "Like I said, it's best we go our separate ways. All we do is disagree."

It annoyed her that he still looked so handsome to her. Even when she was angry with him. "We don't disagree all the time. I came to you because I'm upset with you because you didn't save me a seat beside you. Because you were flirting with that girl, because you're always flirting with other girls."

"Girls flirt with me," he countered. "Nothing I can do about that."

"Sure there is. You could tell girls you're walking out with me," she responded, trying to keep her voice down. If her mother caught wind of their argument, she'd be at

Ginger's side in an instant, intervening, and that wasn't what Ginger wanted. It wasn't what she needed right now. "I didn't want to break up. I just wanted to talk."

"You say I'm not reliable."

"Joe, you're not." Mentally, she counted up how many times he'd been late to pick her up after she worked at Eli's all day. Or didn't come at all. Ginger had tried to talk to Joe about it before, but he was always tired after work and hungry and not receptive to the conversation. To any conversation about their relationship.

And then finally, it had come. The straw that broke the horse's back for her.

The men, led by Bishop Simon, had all gone through the buffet line first, made their plates then scattered to the downstairs rooms to find seats where they could. There were tables set up in every downstairs room in the Fishers' house, but there were also other places to sit like a sofa or a stairstep. The women had gotten into the food line after the men. Ginger had filled her plate and then gone into the parlor, thinking she would join Joe on a bench under the window where she'd seen him sit down. She had assumed he'd saved the place beside him for her.

She'd been wrong.

By the time she had made it to the parlor, one of Edna Fisher's nieces was sitting beside Joe. When Ginger had walked in, Joe hadn't even noticed her. He'd been too busy telling the girl, who couldn't have been eighteen years old, some story about him saving one of his uncle's big contracts. Edna's niece had been giggling and batting her eyelashes as Joe told the story. A story

Ginger had heard before, one that seemed to be getting bigger and better each time he told it. Which was another niggling issue she had with him. She hadn't caught him in an out-and-out lie, but if he embellished stories, did he embellish facts as well?

Ginger had wanted to confront Joe the minute she'd seen him chatting up the girl, but out of respect for Bishop Simon on his special day, she hadn't. Instead, she'd walked out of the room and joined a group of unmarried women in the front hall seated on the staircase. She had kept thinking while she ate that when Joe realized she hadn't joined him, that he would come looking for her. She'd been wrong. Again. After supper, she'd practically had to drag him into the hall to talk to him.

Ginger stood there in front of Joe, her arms crossed. "You said I was your girl," she said quietly.

"Your family doesn't like me," he responded, taking on the tone of a spoiled child. "Your mother barely speaks to me. Your stepbrother Jacob keeps asking me questions hoping to trip me up."

"*Trip you up?* What kind of questions?" she asked.

"About my property at home. What I do for my uncle. Why I left Lancaster. He's just jealous of me because the girls all flock to me." He slid his thumbs under his suspenders, his chest puffing out until he looked like one of her sister Lovey's peacocks. "All the single guys are jealous of me in this town."

She ignored the subject of girls flocking to him. And his hint that maybe he'd ended up in Hickory Grove for some reason other than the one he had given her when they first met—that his uncle had desperately needed him, else his business was going to fail.

"What my mother or Jacob thinks of you shouldn't matter, Joe," she told him, trying to soften her tone. She knew anger wasn't something she should bring into a discussion. That was something her mother had taught her, had taught all of her girls a long time ago. It was just so hard not to be angry with Joe. And hurt. She was more hurt than angry, she thought. And she was feeling foolish to have dated Joe this long. Because he wasn't interested in her. Not interested enough. And he clearly wasn't ready to settle down, otherwise girls *flocking* to him wouldn't be something he'd have brought up.

"I don't want to court you anymore, Ginger." He didn't look at her. "We're not well suited."

"Not well suited?" She flared. "Are we not well suited, or are you just too—" She bit back her next words, words that would not be charitable. Words she would have to pray for forgiveness for later. She crossed her arms so tightly that she was hugging herself. Suddenly she became resigned. "I think you're right, Joe."

"You do?" He looked perplexed, as if people didn't say that to him often.

"*Ya.* We're not well suited," she repeated, purposely not allowing her thoughts to drift to the time she had spent with Eli Saturday. She'd been trying to ignore for weeks the fact that Eli was far more suited to her than Joe. "And we shouldn't be courting. But we can still be friends. *Ya*?" She offered her hand to him. "We're still friends, aren't we?"

Four toddlers ran down the hallway squealing as they chased each other. One was Ginger's little brother Josiah. She pulled in her hand, letting the boys go between her and Joe. When they darted into the living room, she offered her hand to him again.

He looked at her hand, then clasped it awkwardly, giving it a squeeze before letting go.

"Well…" She clasped her hands together, awash with emotions. She knew Joe was right. They weren't a good fit. But it still stung—especially because he broke up with her before she could break up with him. Before she could make that decision. "I've got things to do." She offered a quick, less-than-heartfelt smile. "In the kitchen." She pointed in that direction. "Cleaning up."

Joe just stood there.

Ginger marched off, her chin held high. "It's for the best," she murmured under her breath. "It's for the best." And it was, but by the time she reached the kitchen doorway, she had to stop and wipe the moisture from her eyes.

"There you are, Ginger!" One of the Fisher girls waved to her as she came down the stairs. "Did you hear—"

Ginger ducked into the kitchen, not ready to talk to anyone yet. The kitchen was a flurry of activity with leftovers being wrapped up, dishes being put away and desserts being set out. One of the counters was covered with freshly washed serving dishes. She grabbed her mother's blue baking dish they had brought *schnitz un knepp* in; there hadn't been a spoonful of the pork and dried apple casserole left. Ginger hugged the dish to her, not making eye contact with her sister Bay at the sink, or anyone else. "I'll take this to our buggy, so we don't leave it behind," she said to no one in particular.

She slipped through the back door. It was dark and

cold outside, and it smelled as if it was going to rain any minute. There would be no snow tonight. On the way over to the Fishers', Benjamin had said that they were only expecting a low of forty-five degrees, so he didn't have to worry that the new waterlines that he'd run to the barn might freeze.

Ginger followed the path to the barnyard that was illuminated by solar lights. Her stepfather had them at his harness shop, too. Englishers were always amazed the Amish would use solar power. They didn't understand that things like electricity and phone landlines were about being connected to the world. They were against the *Ordung* because the Amish believed they should hold themselves apart from the non-Amish. But solar power was just like wind power, and not just accepted but encouraged among her people. At least in Hickory Grove.

As Ginger followed the path to the barnyard, she heard male voices and spotted a group of men in the distance gathered at a hitching rail. Someone was smoking a pipe, something she didn't often see. She couldn't tell from a distance who it was. It didn't matter. While smoking was technically against the *Ordung*, it was a small vice. When she was a child, her father had smoked a pipe occasionally, though she had never seen him, only smelled the sweet tobacco.

Ginger hurried toward the long row of buggies, the baking dish clutched to her chest as if it was far more precious than it actually was.

Because of the damp chill, Benjamin had unhitched his gelding and led it inside the barn. She found their buggy easily enough and opened the passenger door.

But instead of just sliding the dish inside, she climbed in. She needed a moment to collect herself before she joined her friends and family. She still couldn't believe that Joe had ended their courtship... Or whatever it had been.

Boys didn't break up with her. She broke up with them. The fact that Joe was the one who had ended their relationship seemed to be what was upsetting her more than anything else. How did he not recognize what a catch she was? What a good person she was? What a good wife she would make?

Ginger fumbled in her pocket for a tissue or a handkerchief. She felt foolish to be crying.

A tap on the buggy's side window startled her.

"Ginger?" came a male voice from outside.

She gripped the seat, unsure for a moment as to what to do. Was it Joe, come to beg her to take him back?

"Ginger?" he called again.

She reached to open the passenger-side door. He beat her to it.

She sat back on the leather buggy seat. "What are you doing out here?"

Eli stuck his head inside. "I came to check on you. You all right?"

She studied him by the light of a kerosene lantern someone had hung on a pole outside the barn door. "I'm fine." She looked down at her hands in her lap and sniffed. "Why wouldn't I be?"

He glanced up into the sky, the broad brim of his wool hat casting a shadow across his face. "Starting to rain." He hesitated. "Would it be all right if I came inside?"

Though Ginger's head was down, she could feel his gaze on her. "Sure," she said. She didn't know that she wanted any company right now, but if she was going to choose someone to be there, it would be Eli.

She moved over to the driver's side. Rather than having a full front bench seat as in her mother's buggy, this new one that Benjamin had built had a split front seat, which allowed one to easily get to the rear benches that faced each other. The buggy was so large that it could accommodate six adults as well as several children.

Eli got inside and closed the door. And suddenly the buggy seemed smaller.

And more intimate.

Which made no sense because she'd been in a buggy with Eli before. Just a day earlier, she'd ridden with him and the children in his buggy to his sister's house to pick up some clothing. Claudia had been doing some sewing for Lizzy and Simon, both of whom seemed to be growing taller every day.

But the children weren't with them now, and that made it different. She'd never been alone with Eli in such a confined space. One that smelled of his clean clothes, shaving soap and something she couldn't quite put her finger on. Something very masculine.

Again, Ginger could feel Eli looking at her.

"You're fine?" he said, his tone suggesting he didn't believe her. "Because I saw you inside in the hallway talking to Joe. You looked upset." He took a breath. "Ginger...you don't have to tell me what happened if you don't want to. But I think I'm a pretty good lis—"

"He broke up with me," she blurted.

He slid back in the seat, seeming as surprised by Joe's action as she was.

"Broke up with you?" Eli repeated. As he took off his hat, raindrops fell on his denim coat. He stroked his clean-shaven chin. When she had first met him, when they had just moved to Delaware from New York, he had still had a beard. It had been a sign of his marital status, though his wife had already passed. But some time ago, he had shaved it off. And had become a single man again.

She gave the slightest nod. "*Ya.* He did. I think it's for the best," she said quietly. She looked down at her hands. "I don't think he ever liked me all that much. He just liked the idea of me."

"Then why are you upset?"

"I don't know. I guess it just…" Why *was* she upset? Hadn't she known it was coming? She opened her hands. "It stings. To be rejected." She was surprised by the words that came out of her mouth. Surprised she would admit such a thing to Eli. Ordinarily, Bay would have been the only person she would have told such a thing.

"*Ya.*" He set the black wool wide-brimmed hat on his knee. "I know exactly what you mean." His eyes twinkled with good humor. "I've been rejected a time or two. As you know." He shook his head. "Everyone in Hickory Grove knows. Everyone in the county. I think word even made it to Lancaster."

Then he smiled at her and suddenly she didn't feel so bad.

"I guess we're in the same situation." He took his time speaking. "And if I'm wrong, say so, but I think you're at the same place I am in my life. I want to marry. I want a partner. And not just to help me care for my children, but to care for me. Care *about* me. I want a partner to care for."

Eli's heartfelt words made her a little uncomfortable, but at the same time she couldn't help but admire him for his honesty. And she was touched that he would share something so personal with her. She didn't know what it was like to be married or even be in love, but she could imagine what it would be like to lose a spouse. She knew what it had been like for her mother.

She sniffed again. "*Ya.* I thought marriage was in my future. I thought Joe and I were well matched. Everyone said so."

"Not everyone," he said. "Not me."

She chuckled. She had suspected all along that Eli hadn't approved of her beau, but unlike her *mam* and sister, he'd kept it to himself.

"And why is that?" she asked boldly.

"I think you know why, but I'll say it. Because Joe didn't treat you the way a man should treat a woman he wants to marry. The way you deserve to be treated, Ginger."

She lowered her gaze. "Which is…what?" she asked, peeking up at him.

"Cherished, respected, adored." This last part he added almost bashfully.

She didn't look away from him this time. "That sounds like something Benjamin would say. He adores my *mam*."

"As a husband should."

"I don't know that every husband adores his wife."

She folded her hands, thinking on the matter. "We marry for many reasons. The most important being because it's God's wish."

"*Ya.* I agree, Ginger. But I also think God wants us to be happy. And to feel loved. By Him, but also by our spouse, by our children. By our community. We don't talk enough about that."

"Can you imagine Preacher Joseph giving that sermon?" she asked, pressing her lips together to keep from smiling. Their new preacher was a good man, one of strong faith, but he was in his seventies and was the soberest soul she thought she had ever known. He tended to lean toward expounding the Old Testament God of wrath. He loved to preach from Deuteronomy, reminding his parishioners of God's threats to the Israelites if they abandoned the covenant he made with them at Sinai. Preacher Joseph also loved the story of Job, always managing to emphasize his trials: the boils, the loss of everything he owned, the death of children.

"*Ya,*" Eli agreed with a conspiratorial smile. "I don't think we'll be hearing much from First Corinthians anytime soon."

Ginger wasn't the best with her Bible knowledge, but First Corinthians she knew. Benjamin often liked to read from Peter's letter during family worship before bedtimes. *Love is patient. Love is kind.* Thinking of those words made a lump rise in her throat. Her mother's husband was such a good man, a good husband, a good father, not just to his boys but to his stepchildren, as well. Ginger had loved her father, but she loved Benjamin too and she admired him for the husband he was to her mother. She wanted a husband like Benjamin. One who would cherish her. Even adore her. But that wasn't something one often saw among the Amish, so she didn't want to get her hopes too high.

Her gaze moved to Eli again. He was just sitting there, watching her by the light that came in through the windshield from the kerosene lantern.

"Well," she said, placing her hands on her knees. "I should get back inside. There are still dishes to be washed."

"*Ya*." Eli tapped his hat on his knee. "And I should get inside and see what the children are up to. If I don't keep an eye on them, they'll be putting slices of pie and slabs of cake in their pockets."

She laughed. "They do enjoy their desserts," she agreed.

"That they do." He sobered, pausing a moment before speaking again. "So, I have a question for you, Ginger. One I best ask before someone else beats me to it again."

She knitted her brows, puzzled as to his meaning. *Beat whom to what?* "What's that, Eli?"

"Ginger…" He swallowed hard, suddenly looking very determined. "May I court you?"

Chapter Eight

Ginger's eyes widened with such surprise that Eli feared he had made a terrible mistake. Had he misread her? All the hours they had spent together when she seemed as if she had enjoyed his company… Had he misinterpreted friendly behavior for one of attraction?

He searched her green eyes with their little specks of brown, trying to read her thoughts.

Why was she hesitating?

Was she trying to think of a way to let him down gently?

Eli wasn't concerned about her hurting him. That was his sister's worry, but it was unfounded. He'd grown a tough skin. He'd asked half a dozen women to walk out with him over the last two years, and not a single one had gone on more than a date or two with him. He wasn't a twenty-year-old boy trying to get a girl to ride home with him from a frolic or sit next to him at supper or a singing. He was a widowed man with a houseful of children and he was asking Ginger to court him with the intention of marrying her.

Ne, he wasn't worried about himself, he was worried about Ginger. Had he upset her? Frightened her? Did she think his request was inappropriate because he was older than she was? It was true she was nine years younger, but he had never thought age mattered. His grandmother had been twelve years older than his grandfather, and they had shared a happy marriage, a happy life together. Or was the fact that he was her employer a problem?

Claudia's words began to bounce around inside his head. A pretty young woman like Ginger would never be interested in an old widowed father of four. That's what Claudia had said. He wasn't handsome enough for the prettiest girl in Hickory Grove. He had never been, not even in his younger years. And he certainly wasn't flashy like Joe Verkler. He didn't wear fancy running shoes or expensive sunglasses. He didn't have blue lights strung on his buggy that lit up after dark.

But the companionship, the laughter, the serious conversations and lighthearted ones he and Ginger had shared had suggested she *was* interested in him. That she saw beyond the threads of gray beginning to show in his hair to who he truly was. What they could be together.

"I… I don't know what to say, Eli." She unfolded her hands and then folded them again.

Had she been staring at the floor, avoiding eye contact, he probably would have apologized for his behavior and taken his leave. But she was watching him. And he could tell she was thinking.

Eli spoke before he lost his nerve. "I know it might seem like this has come out of the blue, Ginger, but—" He hesitated, searching for the right words. He sent a quick prayer heavenward, praying to God to guide him. Because looking into her eyes, he truly believed God meant for this beautiful, kindhearted woman whom his children adored to be his wife. "We've spent a good deal of time together, you and I, over the last… What has it been? Seven weeks since you started watching my children?"

Ginger didn't speak, but she was listening. He took that to mean she wanted to hear what he had to say, and he went on.

"In that time, I feel like I've gotten to know you pretty well and, and…" He fiddled with a sore spot on his palm—a splinter that had not yet made its way to the surface. A carpenter's hazard. "And I think you've gotten to know me pretty well, at least I hope you have." He took a breath, trying to calm his nerves. "We get along well, Ginger. We seem to be able to talk to each other about…about anything and…" He felt like he was making a mess of this, even though for weeks, he'd been rehearsing what he would say to Ginger if he ever got the chance. Practically since the first day he'd come home to find her in his kitchen, supper in the oven, his children happy. And now here the opportunity had presented itself, and he was stumbling and stammering like a boy with his first chin whiskers asking a girl to ride home from a singing for the first time.

Eli took another deep breath, forcing himself to look into her green eyes. "Have I misinterpreted our friendship, Ginger? To think it could be more?"

She wrapped her arms around herself, holding his gaze, and he held his breath, waiting for her to speak. "You've not misinterpreted," she said softly.

He let out a sigh of relief, feeling as if he'd been holding his breath for weeks. "So…would you let me court you? So we can get to know each other better the way a couple should know each other if they're considering—" He stopped, wondering if it was too soon to say it. He didn't want to scare her off. He'd half thought she would flat out turn him down. Like the others. But while he desperately wanted the chance to win her love, he knew he had to be honest with her. Because that was the kind of marriage he wanted, and not just for himself, but for Ginger, too. "If they're considering marriage," he finished, his confidence returning. "And I'll tell you right up front, that's my intention. To marry you, Ginger."

She trembled.

"Are you all right?" He reached out to her but stopped short of touching her hand. He didn't think anyone had seen him get into the buggy with Ginger, but if someone had, he didn't want any assumptions to be made. At their age, the rules of courting were a little more relaxed than if they had been twenty, but there were still rules, especially if they weren't courting.

"*Ya.*" She tightened her arms around herself. "Just chilled all of a sudden."

"I'm sorry. Of course. It's cold out here." He shucked off his coat and put it around her shoulders. "Here you are without even your cloak."

She pressed her lips together, watching him as he eased back into the passenger seat. "*Ya.*"

"*Ya?*" he asked, not sure what she was saying yes to.

"*Ya,* I'll court you, Eli, but—"

Suddenly he began to imagine evenings in front of the fire, reading to the children, playing games, coming together as a family to say evening prayers. He imagined tucking the children into bed and walking down the hallway holding Ginger's hand. He imagined not having to wake each morning to the loneliness he had endured since Elizabeth's death.

"But," Ginger repeated, closing his coat around her. "I'll be honest with you, Eli. I'm not ready to talk about marriage."

And as quickly as that, his dreams faded. He frowned. "You don't want to marry ever, or you don't want to marry me?"

She broke into a smile, chuckling. "Of course I want to marry, Eli. It's only that—"

She exhaled, seeming impatient with him, but it was a good kind of impatient, the kind a wife exhibited with her husband when he said or did something foolish. Eli felt himself begin to relax. She had said yes, that was all that mattered for the moment. "It's only what?" he asked.

"My beau just broke up with me half an hour ago, Eli. It's too soon for me to be talking about marriage to you or anyone else. I think it would be unseemly, don't you? Everyone in the county will be calling me fickle."

"I understand," he said, grinning. He couldn't stop grinning. Ginger said yes. She said she would walk out with him. That was all he wanted—the opportunity to show her how good they could be together. How good a man walking out with a woman should be to her. God was good.

"You sure?" she questioned, sounding an awful lot like his sister. "You understand what I'm saying. I'm willing to enter a courtship, but I don't want to talk about marriage. Not yet."

He nodded, still smiling. "I understand. Nary a word about marriage." He drew his finger across his mouth as if to seal it shut.

Ginger smiled back shyly at Eli, and he felt a rush of warmth run through his body. A rush of hope.

Nettie slid a tray of gingerbread cookies into the oven while Ginger continued rolling out the dough for the next batch. Her stepbrother Ethan, a schoolteacher, was having a cookie sale the first Friday night in December as a fundraiser for Hickory Grove's one-room schoolhouse. With more families moving into the area every year, their building was now barely big enough to hold all of the students. Everyone had agreed that it was time to consider building another school and hiring another teacher—that, or put an addition to the schoolhouse they had now. Either way, they needed money. The community had decided that while they contemplated the best direction to take, the fundraising should begin.

The big news in Hickory Grove was that the holiday cookie sale would be open not only to the Amish but to the Englishers, too. Midsummer, Ethan had proposed the idea of reaching out to their *entire* community for support. After much contemplation and several meetings, the bishops and elders from the different church districts in Hickory Grove had agreed to her stepbrother's proposal. His wife, Abigail, thought they could sell as many cookies as they could bake if they welcomed their English neighbors and encouraged all of the women in Hickory Grove to get out their rolling pins for a good cause. Abigail had even made a huge hand-painted sign announcing the event and planted it in front of the school. Other Amish communities had found that this was an excellent way to raise funds for their schools. One west of Dover held a farm auction every year that was quite successful because the Englishers flocked to such events. Some of the older folks in Hickory Grove had objected to the notion of including Englishers, feeling they would be putting themselves on display for the curious English. Still, in the end, the bishops in Hickory Grove had decided the good outweighed the bad.

It was Bay's idea for their family to start baking early and freeze the cookies so they could contribute plenty to their brother's school. Today, however, she was working in the greenhouse, preparing for the Christmas rush, so she wasn't able to join in. This morning, they were making gingerbread cookies, butter horns and cranberry white chocolate cookies.

"What are you and Eli doing tonight for your first date?" Nettie asked, plucking one hot mitt off and then the other. She'd been pumping Ginger with questions about Eli all morning.

"Are you going to the singing at the Fishers'?" their youngest sister, Tara, asked excitedly.

Taking her time in responding, Ginger chose a cookie cutter in the shape of a cow and began to cut out cookies and slide them onto a baking sheet. She had told everyone in the buggy on the ride home the previous night about her breakup with Joe and about agreeing to court Eli. Her sisters had broken into cheers and giggles. No one seemed to be upset about her breakup with Joe.

Ginger's *mam* had seemed particularly pleased, though she'd been careful not to say too much. She had somehow gotten it into her head that Ginger was inclined to do the opposite of what she wanted, just for the sake of doing it. Which wasn't true. At least not anymore. Dating Joe and working for Eli had changed her perspective. Maybe it was the disappointment of Joe not being what she had hoped he would be, maybe it was the responsibility of caring for Eli's children, but either way, Ginger felt as if she'd matured in the past two months.

"We're a little old to attend singings," Ginger told her younger sister. "Though we may stop by. Eli likes to chaperone the Fishers' frolics."

Edna and John Fisher were the youth leaders for Hickory Grove and did an excellent job of keeping young folks busy while also providing them an opportunity to mingle and get to know each other under proper supervision. Though some Amish around the country practiced *rumspringa*, in Hickory Grove they did not. The church districts were too strict to allow their young men and women the opportunity to possibly dabble in alcohol and smoking, premarital relations and other self-destructive behaviors. Some of the young men occasionally argued that because they weren't yet baptized, it was permissible before they made a formal commitment to live the laws of the Amish life. The bishops in Kent County disagreed. Baptized or not, those behaviors were not permitted.

"So what *are* you two doing then?" Tara pressed. She had been attending frolics for three or four years now but had just begun accepting rides home with boys.

She didn't have a boyfriend yet, so she was fascinated by the whole process.

Ginger dropped another mound of dough that smelled of ginger, cinnamon and molasses on the floured board. Then, taking up the wooden rolling pin that her grandfather had made for her mother as a wedding gift, she began to roll out the dough. Tara moved in beside her at the table and began to measure out the dry ingredients and sift it with an old turn-handle sifter to make the butter horns.

Ginger smiled to herself. As she was leaving the Fishers' last night after the party, Eli had grabbed her hand and pulled her behind the bishop's buggy to whisper, "Would you like to go out on a date with me tomorrow night?" When she'd agreed, he'd asked what she wanted to do, where she wanted to go. She'd told him they didn't have to *go* anywhere. He and the children could come for supper at their house, or she could come to his, and they could play Chinese checkers after they ate.

"That's not a date!" he'd protested.

The way he had said it had made her laugh. At the same time, she'd felt a little shiver of excitement. Her hand felt good in his. Eli had surprisingly soft hands for a carpenter, big and smooth. She thought maybe it was because he used hand lotion out of a bottle he bought at Walmart. He didn't use lard like a lot of men she knew.

"I thought the point was to get to know each other better," she'd argued with him, a twinkle in her eyes. He'd still not let go of her hand. "We don't have to go anywhere to do that."

"We need time without the children," he'd insisted. "Time together alone."

"I don't mind them," she'd told him.

"I mind them," he'd responded, humor in his voice. "Don't get me wrong, you know I love them dearly. But I'm not taking my four children *courting* with me. You deserve my full attention. I'm not saying we'll never do things together with the children. Truth is, most of our courting will be with my children, with your family, with friends and neighbors, but tomorrow night, I want you all to myself. So tell me what you'd like to do." Then his brow had furrowed. "I don't even know how a man my age spends time with a woman, courting. When I courted Elizabeth, we were young." He'd shrugged. "We went to frolics and corn husking parties and—" He had met her gaze, his eyes suddenly widening. "I'm sorry. I shouldn't have done that."

"Done what?" Ginger had asked. She had heard her family loading up the two buggies they'd come in. Her stepbrothers and her brother Jesse had taken one while she and her *mam* and Benjamin and her three sisters and the twin little boys had all ridden together. Benjamin would be ready to go at any minute, and then he'd come searching for her. "What did you do wrong?"

"Mentioned Elizabeth. I shouldn't be talking to the woman I hope will be my future wife about my dead wife."

She'd exhaled, gently pulling her hand from his and tucking it inside her cloak so she wouldn't be tempted to let him hold it again. While Eli's age might give them certain allowances younger folks didn't have, a certain amount of decorum was still expected. "Eli, I don't mind when you talk about Elizabeth. I love that you loved her so much that she still lives inside you." She'd pressed her lips together, wondering what it was about Eli that made her feel comfortable to say what was on her mind.

"Ginger!" Her sister Bay's voice had come from the darkness. "Where are you? Benjamin's ready to go. The littles are falling asleep."

Ginger had looked to Eli, trying to come up with something for them to do. While she'd done plenty of dating, it was always through organized events, mostly with the youth group the Fishers ran. "I have to go home. I don't know what to do. It's not like we go to movies like the Englishers."

"*Ne,* but…" He'd thought for a minute. "We do go out to eat, though. Do you like pizza?"

She had smiled. "I love pizza. I keep telling *Mam* we should learn how to make it. It can't be too hard."

"We'll go for pizza, then. How about that? I'll come to your house to pick you up, but I think I'll get a driver. The place I want to take you to is out on Route 13. Too busy for a buggy at night."

"Ginger!" Bay had called from the darkness outside the puddle of light where Ginger and Eli stood, now sounding annoyed. "She was just here a minute ago," she said to someone.

"I really have to go," Ginger had whispered. She hadn't been able to stop smiling at Eli, because he had been smiling at her. He'd seemed so pleased with himself. He'd looked like Phillip did when the little boy thought he'd managed to snitch cookies from the cookie jar without being caught.

Eli had buttoned up his coat, and Ginger had thought about how it had felt around her shoulders when they were in the buggy earlier. The weight of it had felt like a hug and it had smelled of him.

"Five o'clock?" Eli had asked. "I'll have you home by eight."

"*Ya*," she'd agreed as she backed away from him.

"I can't wait," he'd called after her in a loud whisper.

"We're going out to eat pizza," Ginger said, returning her attention to her sister standing beside her in the kitchen. She dusted a bit of flour off Tara's chin.

"Where?" Tara asked, dumping the last of the dry ingredients into the sifter she held over a big mixing bowl.

Ginger began cutting out more gingerbread cookies. This time she chose the shape of a little house. Later, when they were completely cool, they'd be decorated with homemade orange icing made from orange juice and zest and powdered sugar. "I don't know. Somewhere in Dover."

Tara frowned. "That doesn't sound very safe to me," she said. "There are a lot of Englishers at pizza places with their big cars. You can't leave a horse and buggy in a parking lot in a place like that."

"Eli's hiring a driver," Ginger explained.

"*Mam!*" Tara turned to their mother as she walked into the kitchen carrying a flour sack of something. "Ginger said she's going out for pizza tonight with Eli. I don't think it's a good idea. Benjamin said that when he went to Dover, he couldn't believe how heavy the traffic was. He saw a red car hit a blue one at a stoplight. Those Englishers, they don't pay attention to where they're going."

"I trust Eli to keep our Ginger safe, *Dochtah*. Do I smell cookies burning?" their *mam* asked, sniffing the air.

"*Ne*." At the counter, Nettie was sliding cookies off a baking sheet onto a cooling rack. "Just a cookie I accidentally knocked off the tray into the oven. It's burning on the bottom. I couldn't reach it." She slid the last warm cookie onto the rack. "I'm going to run up to the attic to get some of those old cookie tins. We can freeze the cookies in them. Anything else we need?"

Ginger shook her head and Nettie walked out of the kitchen.

"I didn't find any more dried cranberries in the pantry," their mother said. "We'll have to make the white chocolate and cranberry cookies later in the week after I can get to Byler's. I *did* find some walnuts Lovey gave us, though. We could make snowballs." She held up the cloth bag in her hand. "But someone will have to crack them."

"I can crack nuts when I'm done here," Ginger offered. She loved snowball cookies, which were made with a shortbread recipe and the walnuts. The dough was rolled into balls and baked that way, then rolled in powdered sugar while they were still warm.

"*Ne*, your little brother can do it," her mother answered. "He's been hiding out all morning, avoiding chores."

"Why don't you just come to the singing with us?" Tara's green eyes fixed on Ginger, her pretty face fraught with concern. She'd always been a worrier since she was very young. Their *mam* said everyone in the family had a job to do; Tara's was to worry so no one else had to.

"I told you, we're too old for that sort of thing." Ginger carried the tray of gingerbread cows to the stove for Nettie to put in when the next batch came out. Back at the table, she began to transfer the little gingerbread houses to a clean cookie sheet. "I'm kind of feeling like I am, too."

"You weren't last week when you went to a frolic with Joe," Tara pointed out.

Ginger stiffened but didn't say anything. She continued transferring the cookies. She was still trying to square up the fact that Joe, the man she thought she might marry, had broken up with her. And that Eli had asked her to walk out with him a few minutes later. She couldn't believe she had been so quick to agree. She supposed it was because she was so hurt and disappointed by how things had gone with Joe.

"Tara, can you go find Jesse?" their *mam* asked. "I want him to start cracking these walnuts."

"But I'm mixing up the dough for the butter horns," Tara protested.

"No room in the oven for them until we finish the gingerbread, anyway," their mother responded.

Ginger's sister shrugged. "*Ya*, I can go. I saw him through the window trying to put a leash on that white cat Ethan brought home from school last year."

Tara went to the sink, washed her hands, dried them on her apron and left the kitchen. Ginger's *mam* didn't speak until Tara closed the door behind her. Ginger got the feeling their mother had sent Tara on the errand so she could be alone with Ginger.

"I want you to know that Benjamin and I are very pleased that Eli has asked you to walk out with him and you had the good sense to agree to it."

Ginger picked up the rolling pin and started rolling out another piece of dough, though she already had dough rolled out and ready to be cut into cookies.

"I know you know I didn't approve of Joe from the beginning."

"He's not such a bad person," Ginger said, not wanting to have this conversation with her mother.

"I didn't say he was, *Dochtah*."

An egg timer sitting on the counter went off and her mother opened the oven and pulled out two cookie trays. The kitchen filled with the smell of warm baked gingerbread. "These ready to go in?" She pointed to one of the cookie sheets Ginger had prepared.

"*Ya*. And these." Ginger picked up a cookie sheet of houses from the table beside the one she'd been working on. Their family was so big, with so many adults for meals, that they had two big tables that they configured in various ways, depending on how they were using them. Today they formed an L shape.

"I think you'll find Eli to be kind and patient and very truthful with you. But you already know those things about him, I suspect. And he's fun," her mother added. "Some women like a man more serious, but I think it's important for you to have a husband you can laugh with and play games. Someone who sees your playful spirit. Those times will help you get through the harder ones we all meet."

Ginger cut her eyes at her mother. "No one is talking about marriage right now, *Mam*. I told Eli I'd go out with him. I don't even know why I agreed to it in the first place. It doesn't seem right to be walking out with one man one day and another the next. I don't want people thinking I'm fast." She reached for the rolling pin again.

Her mother was standing there, dressed in a leaf-green dress, her big apron with many pockets over it. Like her daughters, she wore a scarf to cover her hair, tied at the nape of her neck. In her simple clothes with the head kerchief, she looked younger than her years. She looked like she could have been Ginger's sister instead of her mother. Ginger hoped she would age as gracefully as her mother did.

"I guess I said yes because I was upset with Joe," Ginger said as much to herself as her mother.

"Do you mean you *don't* want to walk out with Eli?" Her *mam* took a tone with her that wasn't exactly stern, but it wasn't gentle, either. "Because if that's so, you need to go to him now and call off this date before he pays a driver and carts the children to his sister's so he can take you out."

Ginger stepped back from the table, turning to face her mother. She crossed her arms over her chest. "I'm not saying I don't want to walk out with him. I'm just…"

Her mother waited.

"It's just that…" Ginger exhaled. "I saw my life going one direction, and now it seems as if that's not the way it will go and it's…unsettling."

Her mother smiled warmly. "Life is like that, *boppli*. When I married your father, I thought we would grow old together. That wasn't God's plan for me. But God knew what He was doing, even when I didn't." She opened her arms. "And it all worked out, didn't it? I lost your father, but now he's in Heaven. And I'm happily married to Benjamin. Just because your life doesn't turn out the way you thought it would, that doesn't mean the path you've found yourself on isn't a good path. It's just different."

Ginger nodded, trying to grasp what her mother was saying. Intellectually, she understood, but she was still struggling to reconcile it all in her head and her heart.

"Tell me something," her mother said after a moment. "Do you have feelings for Eli?"

Ginger looked down at her black sneakers.

"Answer my question, *Dochtah*. If you set Joe aside in your mind, do you have room for Eli in your heart? If the answer is yes, then you should put on a clean dress and a freshly starched *kapp* and go have pizza with him. But if you don't think you can be open to the new path God has set in front of you, you have to cancel your date. For Eli's sake and your own."

Ginger stood silent in her mother's warm, sweet-smelling kitchen for a moment. "I do have feelings for Eli. I think I have for some time now." She lifted her gaze to her mother, half-fearful she would judge her for walking out with one man while lying awake at night thinking of another.

But her mother smiled, closed the distance between them and wrapped Ginger in her soft, warm embrace. "Everything is going to be all right, *Dochtah*. Just take a breath, say a prayer and see where this path takes you."

Chapter Nine

"Oh my!" Eli sat back on the bench seat of the van and pressed his hand to his stomach. "I don't think I'll be able to eat for a week. Why did you let me eat five pieces of pizza?"

Ginger slid in beside him and fastened her seat belt, laughing. "I didn't tell you to have five pieces of mushroom pizza. And two root beers. You did that to yourself."

"But no one I know likes mushroom pizza," he explained. "I never get to eat it. Andrew and Simon always want pepperoni." He counted his children off on his fingers. "Phillip likes extra cheese, no meat, no vegetables, and Lizzy only eats the crusts." He waggled his finger at her. "So the fact that we both like mushroom pizza is another good reason why we should be walking out. Who else am I going to share mushroom pizza with?"

Ginger smiled and gazed out the window because she had no answer for that. Why *was* she fighting this? Why was she wrestling with this sense that she and Eli were right for each other? Why was she trying to ignore these feelings she had for him? He clearly felt an attraction to her, though so far, he'd had the good sense not to say anything about it. It was just so obvious that they were well matched. Everyone she cared for thought so: her mother, Benjamin, her sisters, even her friends. So why was she being so stubborn?

So stubborn that she'd almost backed out of their date.

By the time Eli had arrived at her house in the hired van, she had been so nervous that she'd half wanted to cancel, claiming an upset stomach. Her stomach *had* been upset when Eli had come to the door. Since they moved to Hickory Grove, Eli had been coming and going in their house, but he'd never been her suitor before. Her upset stomach must have just been butterflies, though, because by the time Eli had finished chatting with Benjamin about his search for a small pony for his children for Christmas, Ginger had caught her breath and calmed down. She had told herself she was making too much of this whole thing—she was just going for pizza with Eli. Her Eli, whom she saw at least five days a week. Her Eli whom she spent hours with each week in his kitchen playing games and talking.

Still, when he'd asked her if she was ready to leave the house, she'd almost chickened out. But she made herself go because Eli was so excited about going for pizza that she didn't want to disappoint him.

And now she was glad she hadn't canceled because she'd had a wonderful time. None of the boys she had dated had ever taken her out to a restaurant before. It had been an exciting adventure. There had been music playing over loudspeakers: country music, Eli had told her. She didn't know how he knew about English music, but she filed it away in her head to ask him sometime. They'd been seated by a sweet young woman who reminded her of her sister Tara. The girl had strawberry blond hair and dangly earrings that looked like kittens. And then another nice young woman with her black hair in long braids had served them.

Ginger and Eli ordered a large mushroom pizza and large root beers and sat across from each other in a booth. The place was busy, probably because it was a Saturday night, so it had taken a bit of time to get their pizza, but she hadn't minded. Talking with Eli was so easy. So comfortable. With Eli, she didn't have to think about what she was going to say before she said it, and she never regretted her words. With Joe, she had always worried about whether or not she was too outspoken or if he would disagree with what she thought and criticize her for it. That wasn't the case with Eli. He knew who she was, maybe because they had known each other for some time now. But it was more than that. The way he looked at her when she spoke, he seemed truly interested in what she had to say.

"Buckled up?" their driver, Lucy, asked.

Ginger knew Lucy because her family used her services, too. With the heavy traffic and long distances the Amish sometimes had to drive to get to a doctor's appointment or a store, it was common practice for them to hire a driver. It was faster and safer. Lucy, in her late sixties, was a tiny bit of a woman with a helmet of fiery red hair Ginger suspected was dyed. Lucy was a good driver, but a no-nonsense woman and she didn't tolerate tardiness. When she pulled into your driveway at the agreed time, she expected you to be standing on the porch waiting for her. Lucy also wanted to know exactly where she was taking her clients and how long they would be at each stop, and she didn't mind telling you if you broke the rules. She was a local retired schoolteacher who had taught math to seventeen- and eighteen-year-olds. She told Ginger's *mam* that she didn't have to work but that she liked keeping busy. She said that at first, she'd started giving rides to her Amish neighbors over in the Rose Valley area as favors, but transporting those in need had become a full-time job. She was even willing to make longer trips, like out of state to take families to weddings and funerals, though Ginger's family had never used her for that.

Lucy eased out of the parking lot and onto the busy highway. They had one more stop to make. Eli had told Ginger when they got in the van at her house that after they ate, he wanted to go to a local store to get a new ax handle if that was okay with her. Ginger knew the store because they sometimes cut through the parking lot to get to the big box store where they shopped in bulk once a month. The large hardware store Eli needed to go to had intrigued her. They always had rows of small equipment like lawn mowers, snowblowers and gas barbecue grills lined up out front, depending on the season. And they had a huge garden center. In the spring, there were racks and racks of blooming flowers and come fall, there were all kinds of trees and bushes displayed for sale.

"You sure you don't mind stopping?" Eli asked Ginger as if reading her thoughts. "If you're tired, we can go home. I've got an old ax I can use until I get out here again."

Ginger shook her head. "*Ne.* I don't mind stopping." She looked up at him. "Is it all right if I come inside with you?"

She couldn't see his face well in the dark, but she could tell he was smiling at her. "Of course," he said.

"I've never been in here before," she explained, excited now about it.

He rested his arm on the back of the bench seat. He wasn't touching her, but he was close enough for her to feel his warmth and to smell his shaving soap. He'd arrived at her house freshly shaved and his hair, still damp, carefully combed. He was wearing clean, unpatched clothes, his church shoes and what appeared to be a brand-new shirt the color of a robin's egg. She guessed his sister had made it for him. She wondered if Claudia knew he was wearing it out on a date with Ginger. No one had ever said anything, but she had the feeling that Claudia wouldn't approve.

"Never been here before?" he asked, drawing his head back as if shocked. "Well, you're in for a treat. I know it's not very Amish of me, but—" he lowered his voice so that only she could hear him "—this is my favorite store."

Ginger pressed her lips together, suppressing a big smile, and gazed out the window at the sparkling streetlamps and strings of Christmas lights in storefront windows.

Five minutes later, Lucy had parked her minivan and pulled out a paperback novel to read. She always had a book with her.

"Twenty minutes," Eli told Lucy as he opened the sliding door to the van. "That okay?"

Lucy reached for a big paper cup from a fast-food place and took a sip from the straw. "I'll be right here."

Eli stepped out into the dark parking lot and offered his hand to Ginger.

She hesitated. Usually the drivers they used had a step stool to get in and out.

Before she could decide whether to take Eli's hand, he grasped hers.

She stepped down out of the van, distracted by the feel of Eli's warm, strong hand. Just then, a gust of wind kicked up, and he let go of her to grab his hat. She laughed as the wind whipped at her heavy cloak.

"Ready?" he asked.

She nodded, and they walked side by side toward the glass door. When they got close, it opened automatically.

"Let me grab that ax handle, and then I have a surprise for you. Something I suspect you'll like."

She looked up at him. "What?"

He shook his head. "It wouldn't be a surprise if I told you, now, would it?" They walked past a customer service desk. At the back wall, they took a right. There was so much to see that Ginger couldn't take it all in. She saw light fixtures and sinks and flooring. The store was busy with customers, Englishers dressed in fuzzy coats and thick colorful sweaters and bright hats with pom-poms on top.

"Let's see," Eli said. "We're looking for aisle RW," he said. "Here we go. Ax handles."

Ginger followed Eli, turning her head to watch a woman in a puffy white coat walk past them, pushing a cart. In the front of the cart was a tiny white dog dressed in a puffy coat that looked remarkably like the owner's. Ginger had to press her hand to her mouth to keep from giggling. Both had short spiky white hair on top of their heads and a red barrette.

Eli caught Ginger gaping and grabbed her hand, leading her down the aisle. As they walked, their gazes met. Eli's blue eyes were dancing. He'd seen the dog with the coat and hair barrette, too.

"Here we are," Eli said, coming to stand in front of a display of axes and ax handles. "Let's see, hickory double-bit, fiberglass, forged steel." He squeezed her hand before letting go and then began picking up the ax handles one at a time.

Ginger stood there watching him, still feeling the warmth of his hand on hers. She couldn't believe how relaxed she felt with Eli in this new role as his girlfriend. It was as if they had been a couple for weeks, months. Years. Being with him was just so easy, so comfortable. Standing beside him, watching him weigh the differences between one ax handle and another, she could see herself at his kitchen table as his wife, riding to church on Sunday mornings in his buggy. She could see herself growing old with Eli, raising a family with him.

Interestingly enough, even though she'd been determined she and Joe would marry, she had never seen those things in her mind's eye with him. It was almost as if the *idea* of Joe had been what had attracted her—his good looks, the way folks made a fuss over him.

"I think I'll go with the hickory," Eli said to her, holding it up. "What do you think?"

"I don't know a thing about ax handles."

"Maybe not, but I've found that most women have

an opinion on just about everything." He smirked. "And they're usually right."

"The hickory." She pointed to the ax handle in his hand. "I'd get the hickory."

"Hickory it is, then." He reached for her hand and took it and then looked at her. "Is this all right? My holding your hand?"

Suddenly in the busy store, Ginger felt as if she and Eli were the only ones there. She gazed into his eyes. "I don't know that Bishop Simon would approve," she said, surprised by the shyness in her voice. "But...it feels right."

His smile was gentle. "It feels right to me, too, Ginger." He held her gaze another moment longer and then tugged on her hand. "Okay, shopping done. Now your surprise. Well, it's not exactly a surprise. I'm sure you've seen such things before, but they have a nice Christmas shop here. Lizzy loves it."

She let him lead her back down the aisle they'd come. "You think Lizzy and I like the same things?"

"You both like chocolate chip cookies without walnuts," he pointed out.

She rolled her eyes at him as they walked through a doorway into the area that was the garden shop. "*Ya*, but—" She stopped where she was and gazed around her. The whole room was filled with Christmas trees twinkling with white lights and colored lights, some flashing, some blinking, some as steady as the stars. There were Christmas lights everywhere and decorations galore. She turned around slowly, not knowing where to look first. There were big Santas popping out of fake chimneys and little birds on garland strings.

Around the artificial trees were buckets of ornaments that looked like foxes and shoes and candy canes and cats. The Christmas trees were big and small, most green, but one a sparkly white. And they were covered in lights and ornaments.

Still holding Ginger's hand, Eli led her through what seemed like a forest of Christmas trees. "This is my favorite one," he told her. He stopped in front of a tree decorated with soft, unblinking white lights. The whole tree was decorated in what looked like homemade ornaments: cookie cutouts, pine cones painted with white tips to look like snow, sticks of cinnamon glued together and tied with a little red bow.

Ginger reached out and touched one of the bundles of cinnamon sticks and it spun slowly. It had a little white tag attached to it. She read the tag. "Five dollars?" she exclaimed.

An employee stacking boxes of purple lights looked at her.

She lowered her voice, turning her back to the Englisher. "They're charging five dollars for two sticks of cinnamon and a bow. Do you know what that would cost to make?" She went on before he could answer. "Bay needs to see this tree. She could sell ornaments like these in her garden shop." She looked up at Eli. "Those are just pine cones sprayed with a clear coating and a little white paint."

He was smiling at her.

She smiled back and then said suspiciously, "What?"

He shook his head. "Nothing."

"Why are you looking at me like that?"

"You always say Bay is the businesswoman of the family, but I think you have a mind for it, too."

"Me?" She drew back.

"I've seen you working the cash register at Benjamin's harness shop. You're good with the customers."

"I usually work in the back." Before she had started working for Eli, she'd often worked shifts in Benjamin's shop, repairing bridles and such. She liked doing leatherwork. It was less delicate than needlework, and she liked the smell of freshly cut leather.

"I know you do. I'm just saying you're smart, Ginger."

Smart. She didn't know if anyone had ever said that to her. In her family, she had always been the pretty one. Bay was the smart one. She liked that Eli saw that in her rather than just focusing on her looks.

"Thank you," she said.

He looked down at her. "For what?"

She looked around. "For the pizza and soda. For this. I've had a really good time with you tonight, Eli."

"A good enough time to do something again with me? There's a chicken and dumpling supper over at Seven Poplars' schoolhouse Tuesday night. A fundraiser for Abe Zucker's little one. Been in and out of the hospital for weeks. Want to go with the children and me?" He raised an eyebrow. Like his hair, they were a dark red, which seemed to make his eyes look even bluer.

"I'd like that," she whispered.

They went to a cash register to make their purchase and then out into the cold night. Walking hand in hand with Eli across the parking lot, Ginger thought to herself this might have been the best evening she'd ever had in her life.

* * *

Eli made his way slowly toward his back porch, trying to settle himself. Molly seemed to sense his mood and trotted beside him, rather than circling him and barking the way she usually did. He hadn't had a good day at work. The client had stopped by to see the progress of his house and had gotten into a long, agitated discussion with Eli about what he liked and didn't like about the custom work Eli was doing for him. Mostly it was about what he didn't like. Eli had notes and drawings, which had been preapproved before he'd started the paneled woodwork that would go over the fireplace and flank it. He'd done exactly what the client had asked, and now the client had changed his mind. The whole interaction had frustrated Eli. Though he tried hard not to be prideful, he knew he had created a beautiful fireplace. The client didn't understand wood as a medium and what could and could not be done with the type of wood he had chosen. Now Eli would have to have a talk with his boss to see what was to be done. If the client wanted the whole mantelpiece and surrounding wainscoting removed and remade, Eli would do it. But it would mean a week of additional work and he didn't believe he or Ader should be penalized for the client's fickleness.

At the back steps, Eli stopped, and Molly dropped down beside him. The dog peered up at him expectantly.

Eli tried to soothe his irritation. He'd been gone all day; his children deserved better than a cranky *dat*. And what would Ginger think if he came into the house with a sour face? He took another step and stopped.

What would she *think*?

He would hope she would think that he'd had a bad day. Everyone had one occasionally. If this was going to work, if he and Ginger were going to marry, and he hoped with his entire heart that would be the case, she had to know him as he was. Yes, he was normally a positive person, a man that reminded himself every day of God's goodness. But at times, everyone got tired, frustrated and stuck in a loop of negative thinking. Being married meant respecting, even loving, their partner for all the good things about them and the not-so-good things, as well.

Inside the mudroom, Eli removed his work boots, his coat and his hat and walked into the kitchen in his stocking feet. The room smelled of the fire in the fireplace and the delicious aroma of baking chicken and fragrant herbs.

Ginger was seated in the chair that was to the right of his chair at the kitchen table. The chair that had become hers. And she was darning socks… One of his socks.

She looked up at him and smiled. "How was your day?"

He hesitated, his emotions suddenly a jumble. There was something about seeing her with his sock in her lap that tugged at his heartstrings. Tugged at them even more than her beautiful face, her beautiful smile. He shrugged. "Not the best. Yours?"

She lowered the darning to her lap. She was wearing a dark blue wool scarf over her hair and tied at the nape of her neck rather than a prayer *kapp*. He liked seeing her in his kitchen in a scarf because it symbolized her comfort in his home.

She nodded slowly. "Sorry you didn't have a good day. Want to tell me about it?"

"Maybe later," he responded. "But right now, I'd rather hear about your day."

"All right. Hmm. Let's see," she said. "I had a nice day. We all did. After Andrew and Simon went to school, I did laundry, fixed the torn hem on Lizzy's green dress, helped Phillip make piglets out of cardboard tubes from the paper-towel roll, washed dishes and…made supper."

"And darned socks." He pointed at the darning basket.

"And darned socks."

He nodded. "Smells good in here. Chicken?"

"Turkey breast. Tara's recipe. You rub it with olive oil and sprinkle fresh chopped rosemary on it. We have baskets of rosemary. *Mam* grows it in her garden and Bay's been using it in some of her floral arrangements she's selling at the garden shop."

He walked over to the stove to see red-skinned potatoes bubbling on a back burner. He turned and leaned against the sink, sliding his hands into his pockets. In a minute, he'd go wash up, but right now, he just wanted to stand here and be with Ginger. "What time is someone coming for you? Can you stay for supper?"

She picked up her darning again and smiled teasingly. "I had supper with you last night."

"But not here." He watched her capable hands make short work of the hole in the toe of one of his socks. "That was a fundraiser, and we were surrounded by fifty other people. Including my children." He glanced around, realizing he hadn't heard a peep from one of them since he got home. "Speaking of my children, where are they? It's awfully quiet around here. You lock them in the cellar?"

She gave him a look. "I did not. Let's see. Andrew is cleaning up a mess he made in the upstairs bathroom sink, trying to wash his marbles. I sent Simon to the smokehouse to get a bit of bacon for the lima beans. I would guess he stopped to play with the kittens in the barn. I'm surprised you didn't see him when you put the horse up. And Lizzy and Phillip are doing puzzles in the living room. We made them from a cardboard box. Kitten puzzles. That's what they're supposed to be. My drawing isn't the best."

He smiled, feeling himself begin to relax. She was always doing fun things like that with the children, making puzzles from cardboard, toys from scraps. Things he would never think to do. He loved that she was here to do those little activities. "You didn't answer my question. Can you stay for supper? And maybe a quick game of Chinese checkers?"

"Bay's been teasing me. She says marriage would never work for us because all we would do was sit around and play games. She says nothing would ever get done and the children would have to live on cookies you bought at Byler's."

He laughed. That sounded like something Bay would say. "You and your sister are talking about us marrying, are you?" he dared. "She thinks you ought to marry me?"

Ginger lowered her gaze to her darning and pushed the needle through the wool sock. "I shouldn't have told you that. It will put ideas into your head."

Her tone was playful, but he also got the impression that she hadn't discounted the idea. They hadn't been walking out together for long, but if they were right together, they were right together. The amount of time they courted didn't matter. And with every passing day, he was more certain that they *were* meant for each other. He'd been praying for so long for God to send him a wife. Now he had come to believe that God had meant for him to bump into Ginger and her mother at Byler's that day so that she could be here caring for his children while he worked. While they got to know each other. And now here they were.

"I told you from the beginning that was my intention, Ginger." He took a step toward her. "I told you I wanted to marry you."

She was quiet.

"I think we're meant for each other," Eli went on. "We get along well. The children love you and…" He suddenly felt tears sting the backs of his eyes. He thought of his Elizabeth and the love they shared and realized that he loved this woman, too. What a gift from God, he thought. To love two women in a lifetime. The question was, could Ginger love *him* one day? Because he'd made up his mind long ago. Men and women married for many reasons, and not always for love, but after the love he had shared with Elizabeth, he couldn't imagine a loveless marriage.

"The children love you, Ginger, and I love you," Eli pressed on, having no idea what had made him say such a thing in the middle of his kitchen on a Wednesday evening.

Ginger rose, setting the darning in a basket on the kitchen table. She walked slowly toward him and he watched her, looking for signs that he had ruined everything by talking about marriage too soon. By making proclamations of love when they'd only been courting less than a week.

"I thought the plan was to wait awhile before we talked about this," she said.

He brushed his hand across his mouth. "You're right. That was the plan. I'm sorry. It's only that I—" He glanced away. "I didn't mean to—" He returned his gaze to her. She was standing very close in front of him. So close that he could have kissed her. So close that he wanted to kiss her. But he restrained himself. He wasn't interested in casual dating. Or kissing a woman he would not marry. He prayed silently now that he would get to kiss Ginger one day, when they were man and wife.

"It's all right, Eli," she said to him. "It's only that… that I'm not ready to talk about…love yet."

"Because of Joe?" It came out of his mouth before he had time to think. "Because you were in love with him?"

The smile she offered was so sweet, so kind, and also a smile that gave him hope. There was something about the way she was looking at him that made him think maybe she really would agree to be his wife. Maybe not today, maybe not tomorrow. But one day.

"Joe doesn't matter anymore, because I'm not walking out with Joe. I'm walking out with you, Eli. But I need more time. I want to be sure this is right. That you're the man I'm meant to marry."

"So what I'm hearing," he said, lightening the mood, "is that this old man might have a chance with you?"

She smiled up at him. "This old man just might."

Chapter Ten

By the time Ginger walked down the lane from the house to the garden shop, the parking lot was packed with buggies, cars and trucks. Despite the cold temperatures and threat of a wintry mix, it seemed as if everyone in Hickory Grove, Amish and English, had turned out for Bay's first annual Christmas wreath-making workshop.

Ginger had been sent to the kitchen to grab another big tin of peanut butter thumbprint cookies. Bay and Joshua were serving cookies, hot chocolate and hot cider after their workshop, and the turnout was higher than they'd expected. Bay was worried they would run out. Tara had fussed that they would be giving away a lot of the cookies they had made for the schoolhouse cookie sale, but Bay explained that it was good business to give away a few cookies in the hope folks would come to the sale the next weekend. She'd put up signs in the harness shop and her garden shop advertising the fundraiser, and she suspected they'd sell every cookie the women in Hickory Grove could bake for the cause.

As Ginger cut across the gravel parking lot that served both the garden shop and the harness shop, she spotted Eli's buggy and smiled to herself. She was looking forward to seeing him and the children; she missed them on the Saturdays when they didn't get together. Ginger was amazed by how easily her life had fallen into place once she had surrendered to allowing God to guide her. With Joe, she'd been constantly trying to force her will on God and Joe, trying to convince them both that she and Joe were meant to be together. Now she knew that she was wrong. And she was thankful she had been, because she was so happy with Eli, happy in a way she doubted she could ever have been with Joe.

For the first time in her life, Ginger felt like she was a better person when she was with someone else than when she was alone. And that someone else was Eli. It was just so easy to talk with him, to be with him. He made her want to be a better person, a woman of stronger faith with more patience. And she loved the days she spent with his four little ones while he was at work. She had fallen in love with them. And now she was beginning to realize that though she didn't know what it felt like to fall in love, she suspected she had. Or was. She just hadn't taken the time to process it.

Exhaling puffs of frosty breath, Ginger hurried toward the garden shop door. Bay had decorated it with one of her generous wreaths made from boxwood branches, pine cones and a big red gingham bow. The door was outlined with white Christmas lights that were powered by one of the generators that ran the shops. There had been talk as to whether Bay was getting too fancy, adorning the shop with twinkle lights. However, because many of their customers were English, Benjamin, as the head of the family, had approved the decorations and said that if their bishop had a problem with it, he could talk to him.

Bells jingled as Ginger stepped through the doorway in the shop. The building was barely more than a shed and lit brightly with more Christmas lights. The greenhouse and garden shop were already so successful that Bay and Joshua had plans to build a new shop in the spring, one much bigger than this temporary building they were using.

Joshua's wife, Phoebe, greeted Ginger at the door. She'd been tasked with checking families in before sending them in the direction of the greenhouse, where Bay would be giving her workshop on wreath making. They'd spent the whole morning moving poinsettias and fresh table arrangements to make room for those attending the workshop. They would be using the tables that usually displayed plants as a work surface. Bay had also borrowed some chairs from the church wagon. Ordinarily, the tables and chairs were used for church events, weddings and such. However, Bay had convinced the elders to let her use them for the event with the promise to deliver the wagon to her brother Ethan's house in time for him and his wife, Abigail, to get everything set for the next church Sunday.

When Ginger walked in, Phoebe opened her eyes wide as if to say "Help me! Things are crazy here!"

Which they were. The shed, smelling of pine boughs and cinnamon and nutmeg, was packed with friends and neighbors and familiar and unfamiliar English faces. It was standing room only. Bay stood near the checkout counter, trying to usher folks past her and into the connecting greenhouse.

The doorbells jingled, and an English woman in a long skirt, leading a little girl by the hand, walked in. "My, it's bitter out there," she remarked. The woman and child were wearing brown, fuzzy coats with red scarves around their necks that made them look like the teddy bears Ginger had seen in stores.

"Amber and Taylor Crouse," the woman said to Phoebe. "We preregistered." She glanced around. Her cheeks were bright red from the cold, and she was wearing lipstick that matched. "This is so much fun. Doing a craft at a real Amish farm. We just moved into the area. We're across the street from the schoolhouse, the old Baker farm." She pointed in the general direction.

Phoebe smiled and made a mark on her notepad. "Good to have you with us. Head that way, and someone will help you find a spot at a table in the greenhouse. We're going to get started in about fifteen minutes."

"Is there going to be a tour of the farm? I know it's dark, but we'd love a tour."

"Sorry, no tours," Phoebe said sweetly.

Ginger watched the woman and her daughter make their way toward the greenhouse. Bay had finally gotten the crowd in motion, and there was now space in the shed to move around a little. There were still folks stopping to talk to each other. Eunice Gruber was standing by the checkout counter, talking loudly about someone's trip to the dentist. Probably not one of her own family members. Eunice always knew all of the gossip in Hickory Grove. Good and bad.

"With all these preregistrations, we can only take

one more walk-in," Phoebe told Ginger. "Joshua only made up frames for thirty-five wreaths."

"I just put three more together, so we can do thirty-eight, but any more than that and we won't have enough greenery anyway," Joshua said, walking toward them. He was dressed as if he had just been outside, in a heavy denim coat and a navy blue knit cap pulled down over his ears. "We're getting another shipment Monday morning." When he reached his wife, he frowned at her. "I brought you a stool so you would sit on it." He pointed at the stool next to the door. "You've been on your feet all day. You need to rest." He took her hand and led her toward the stool. "Sit, wife."

Phoebe obediently dropped to the stool.

"Joshua!" Bay called from her post at the checkout counter. "Could you grab a couple more chairs from the church wagon outside? Mrs. Carter's grandmother needs one. At the end of the first table. They're just making one wreath, but I wasn't expecting so many people to come from each family."

"Great, isn't it?" Joshua called back. "I'll take care of it, Bay. It's fine. We've got plenty more chairs, and I dug up some more floral wire and pine cones." He set his hand on the door to go outside. "Ginger, could you please make sure my wife stays put for a few minutes? She's done too much today."

Phoebe laughed. "I've not done too much. There's been a lot to do today. We had to get ready for this evening, and customers were still coming and going."

Joshua looked at Ginger as he walked out the door. "She's done too much," he repeated, then closed the door behind him, the bells jingling overhead.

Phoebe met Ginger's gaze. "I can't get him to understand that there's nothing wrong with me. I'm not sick or hurt." She rested her hand on her rounded belly. In the last few weeks, she'd really popped out. While it was poor manners among the Amish to speak publicly of pregnancy, there could be no doubt in anyone's mind that Joshua and Phoebe were expecting their first baby. "I keep telling him there's nothing more natural. I feel wonderful. You'll see when you and Eli are married," she added softly, her eyes twinkling.

Ginger was surprised by the lump of emotion that rose in her throat. She looked away. She hadn't really ever thought that much about having babies of her own. Of course she had always known she wanted children, if God was willing to so gift her and her husband. But now the idea of having a child of her own body was something she was thinking about more and more often. It wasn't something she had ever thought about with Joe, but with Eli… This was somehow different. Of course, Andrew, Simon, Phillip and Lizzy would become her children when she and Eli wed. And she was now thinking in those terms: when they wed, not if. But having their own children together seemed like something that would only add to the close knitting of their new family.

Ya, she wanted to marry Eli. But she was pushing him to be patient. And herself. Marriage was for a lifetime, a big commitment before God and their community, and Ginger knew she had to be absolutely sure that Eli was meant to be her husband and she his wife. There had been whispers among the younger unmarried women in Hickory Grove that Ginger was making a mistake considering marrying a man with children, a man so much older than she was. One of the girls had piped up with a giggle that it would be like marrying your father. Tara had told her she'd overheard several girls talking at Spence's Bazaar about it. None of them could understand how Ginger could let a boy like Joe Verkler get away.

Eli's age wasn't an issue for Ginger. He never seemed too old or fatherly in any way to her. And despite his comments about his gray hair and wrinkles, she found Eli attractive. Not in the way she had found Joe attractive. Joe was so handsome he was almost pretty. Granted, Eli had a few lines etched on his face, but to her, they were tiny lines of experience, of knowledge. And the twinkle in his eyes, the way he looked at her when he thought she wouldn't notice, made her feel weak in the knees in a way Joe's gaze never had.

The bells jingled as the door opened again, breaking Ginger's reverie. "I best get these cookies to the refreshment table. You know how Tara worries," Ginger told Phoebe. "She wants everything laid out just so. I tried to tell her we could set up the snacks while folks were making their wreaths, but she wouldn't have it."

Phoebe got up off the stool. "I'll be in to help in a few minutes. Just a few more folks to arrive."

"I think the plan is to start on time, whether everyone who's registered is here or not," Ginger said over her shoulder as she walked away. "You best sit down before your husband comes back in."

Phoebe cut her eyes at Ginger. "My husband likes to pretend he's tough, but I know better. He's soft and sweet in the middle." She smiled the smile of a woman in love with her husband, her new family and her new life. A distant cousin to Ginger on her mother's side, Phoebe had had a hard go of it in Pennsylvania where she'd grown up. She'd loved a man and nearly lost everything, including her son, but all had changed the previous year when she'd arrived on the Millers' doorstep in need of shelter and a new chance at life.

As she made her way to the greenhouse, Ginger greeted friends and neighbors, having to talk loudly to be heard above the cacophony of voices speaking English and Pennsylvania *Deitsch*. And one English man trying to talk in German to one of Ginger's stepbrothers who had taken over for Bay, trying to usher everyone to their seats so the workshop could begin.

As Ginger entered the greenhouse, she began to unfasten her cloak with one hand. It was quite a bit warmer inside; she'd have to shed her cloak. Her sweater over her dress would be enough.

"Ginger!"

Ginger saw a flash of denim and barn boots as Phillip launched himself against her, wrapping his arms around her legs.

"Easy, Phillip!" Ginger cautioned in Pennsylvania *Deitsch* as she laughed, trying to keep her balance.

"*Dat* said I could come get you. He said you were going to help us make our wreath. Are you going to help us?" The little boy bounced on his toes and hugged her again.

"Where is your *dat*?" she asked, gazing out over the crowd.

Phillip spun around. "I don't know. He's here somewhere."

Ginger laughed. "Let me put these cookies down and

we'll look together." But as she headed for the refreshment table set up in the back and decorated with white and red poinsettias, Phillip took off in the opposite direction with one of the neighbor's boys.

"There you are," Tara called to Ginger in Pennsylvania *Deitsch* as she approached the table. She was busy setting out napkins. "I don't know if we have enough cups for the hot cider." She looked up. "Do you think we should serve cold cider too?"

"I think just the hot cider will be fine," Ginger said, setting down the tin of cookies.

"I don't know. Maybe we should have cold. I'll have to get more cups. I think we have paper ones up at the house," Tara fretted.

"Here. Can you put my cloak with yours?" Ginger asked, handing it across the table to her sister.

"*Ya.*" Tara took it and turned around to lay it over a chair. "Oh, I almost forgot. Someone was looking for you."

"Eli? I know. Phillip—"

Tara turned back. "*Ne*, it was Joe."

Ginger made a face. "Joe? Verkler?"

"*Ya.* He was here a little while ago asking for you." She held up some small napkins. "You think these are okay? I thought we had bigger napkins at the house, but I couldn't find them."

Ginger made a face. "What does Joe want with me?"

Tara shrugged. "I don't know. I heard he broke up with that girl from Seven Poplars." She leaned closer and whispered, "Maybe he wants to get back together with you."

Ginger dropped her hands to her hips and laughed. "Get back together with me? *That's* not going to happen."

"You might have to tell him that yourself," Tara said. She nodded in the direction over Ginger's right shoulder. "There he is," she whispered.

Eli stood talking to Lynita Byler and nodded as if he heard every word she said. As the older woman went on about how she'd chased a fox from her henhouse, his gaze fell on Ginger's back. She was standing at the refreshment table talking with Tara. Ginger was wearing a rose-colored dress and navy blue knit cardigan. Her prayer *kapp* covered her blond hair, but tiny tendrils had escaped and curled at the nape of her neck. He couldn't hear what they were saying; Lynita was getting hard of hearing, which meant she thought everyone else was, too. He smiled and nodded as he watched Ginger. Tara was directing her to look at something or someone.

Eli slid his hands into his pants pockets as he casually turned to see what Ginger was now looking at. Not what. But *whom*.

Joe Verkler.

It took Eli by surprise. To see Joe and his Ginger in the same room. To see Joe looking at her the way he was.

Eli suddenly felt sick to his stomach.

Could he really compete with a young man that handsome, a man still in his twenties who could probably chop wood all afternoon without stopping?

Eli's gaze shifted to Ginger again. Then to Lynita, who had wandered on to the subject of her grandson and his fondness for golden raisin cookies. "Where are those children?" Eli muttered, shaking his head. "I best find them." He nodded politely. "Good to talk to you, Lynita."

"*Ya*," she agreed. "You let me know if you have trouble with foxes in your henhouse," she called after him as he walked away.

He raised his hand. "Will do."

By the time Eli reached the refreshment table, Ginger was talking to Tara again. When Ginger saw him, she broke into a wide grin. "There you are."

"Here I am," he said, glad he'd taken the time to change not just his shirt but his trousers, too. Ginger was as pretty as ever. Her cheeks were pink, maybe from the cold.

She slid her arm casually through his, taking him by surprise. They held hands in private: when they were out on a date, like when they'd gone for pizza, and sometimes at the table when they were playing Chinese checkers. But only when the children weren't in the room. This was the first time he could recall them ever touching this way in front of anyone, and it made his heart swell. He was pleased that she found it natural to take his arm. He was equally pleased that she would do it in front of others. In front of Joe. He knew he shouldn't feel this way. He wasn't in a competition with Joe for Ginger's heart. He couldn't compete with a flashy young man like Joe, nor did Eli want to. But just the same, her touch made him happy. It was as if she was announcing to the world that he was her beau. That she chose him.

"I asked Phillip where you were," Ginger said. "But he couldn't remember."

"Up front, on the left." He met Tara's gaze. She was watching them. He nodded hello and she nodded back.

"Hello! Thank you for coming tonight!"

Eli glanced over his shoulder to see Bay standing in front of the room, trying to get everyone's attention.

"If everyone could find a place!" Bay practically shouted.

Several people were trying to shush their neighbors, and one of the young men, maybe even Joe Verkler, whistled between his teeth.

"Hey, listen up!" someone hollered.

Suddenly the entire group lowered their voices.

"If you could find a place, we'll get started. Each family needs to find a spot with one of these." Bay held up a round wire frame. "You're going to use this frame to form your wreath."

"Are you going to help us?" Eli asked Ginger. "The children are excited about making a wreath with you."

"Let me help Tara get these cookies out and then I'll be over." Ginger's gaze met his and he felt himself relaxing. He had nothing to worry about, least of all Joe Verkler. Ginger cared for him. He could see it in her green eyes when she looked at him.

"I'll try to keep them busy until you get there." He reluctantly released her arm. "And try not to mess up the wreath."

She flashed him a smile and Eli felt as if he was walking on clouds as he crossed the room and joined Phillip, Andrew and Lizzy at the table next to Claudia and two of her girls.

"Ginger coming to help us?" Andrew asked.

"In a minute," Eli assured him as he took a spool of

floral wire from Phillip's hand. "We're going to need that in a minute, *Sohn*."

"Ginger's coming?" Andrew repeated.

"She sure is."

As Eli said it, he caught, out of the corner of his eye, his sister watching him. Her arms were crossed over her chest. As if she wanted to say something. Eli sighed. "What?" he said softly.

"I didn't say anything," she responded.

"*Ne*, but you want to." He met her gaze. They were the same height, he and Claudia. Maybe that was how she had remained so formidable in his mind, even after all these years. After their mother died, it was Claudia he'd always worried about displeasing. Not their father.

"I saw her flirting with you right in front of everyone."

Eli looked straight ahead. Bay was talking again, explaining how to choose longer pine branches to make the base of the wreath.

When Eli didn't respond to his sister, she went on. "You know why she's doing that, don't you? That old boyfriend of hers. He's here tonight."

Eli cut his eyes at his sister. "Ginger and I are walking out together," he said softly. "Old boyfriends don't matter anymore."

Claudia sighed. "I know I've said this before, but I'll say it again. I think you're naive, Eli. She's playing with you. I don't blame her. It's what young girls do. But you, you're old enough to see through it. And if you don't, I'm afraid you're going to get hurt."

Eli took a deep breath and exhaled. Claudia went on talking, even as Bay started giving instructions again.

But he didn't hear either of them because he was too busy making up his mind that tonight was the night. He was going to ask Ginger to marry him and put an end to this nonsense with his sister.

An hour later, Eli had a beautiful wreath sitting on the table in front of him. Thanks to Ginger, who had not only tied the bow and added several sprigs of holly with red berries, but had also saved the day when she managed to reattach part of the greenery that fell off when Andrew accidently cut the wrong piece of wire.

"*Dat*!" Lizzy cried. "Can I have a cookie? Ginger *shaid* there was cookies."

Looking for Ginger, who had just walked away, disappearing into the crowd, Eli clasped his daughter's hand and led her toward the refreshment table. "*Ya*, one cookie. But that's it. You had cookies at home before we left." They were almost to the table when Eli spotted Ginger. He looked around, saw Simon. "Get a cookie for your sister," he told his son. "Keep her right here. I'll just be a minute." Eli gave Lizzy a nudge toward her brother and then slowly made his way across the greenhouse to where Ginger was busy stacking half-used spools of wire.

"Thank you for helping us tonight. I think we have the prettiest wreath," he told her.

"I don't know." She looked up at him. "Did you see the one someone made with all the pink plastic doughnuts on it?" Her mouth twitched with amusement. "I guess she brought them with her."

"I did not." He laughed, now stalling for time. He'd planned what he wanted to say, but now that the time had come, he was suddenly nervous. He knew that

Claudia, though well-meaning, didn't know Ginger. She didn't know how kindhearted she was. What a good parent she was to his children. How perfect she was for him. All Claudia saw was the pretty face; she couldn't get past that.

"Ginger…" He took a breath. "Can I talk to you for a minute?"

She lifted a blond eyebrow, as she began putting the rolls in a cardboard box. "You are talking to me."

He glanced around. The greenhouse was still full of people. Everyone was visiting with friends and neighbors, having a cookie and a drink and in no hurry to go home.

"In private," he said, grabbing her hand and ducking behind a tall arrangement of poinsettias. Anyone who looked closely might be able to tell they were back there, but it would at least give them some semblance of privacy.

"What's gotten into you?" Ginger asked, laughing.

He was still holding her hand. He took a deep breath and looked into her eyes. "Ginger Stutzman, will you marry me?"

At first Ginger seemed surprised. Then her face softened. "I thought we were going to wait a little while before we talked about this," she said quietly.

"I know. I know you said that, but… I can't help myself. Making the wreath together, seeing you with the children. They all love you so much. And…" He pressed his lips together and forged on. "You already know I'm in love with you," he said softly. "So…"

She took his hand between hers. "Eli, please. I'm not ready. I still need some time to get to know you. To—"

"It's Joe Verkler, isn't it?" Eli interrupted, taking his hand from hers.

She looked up at him, her forehead wrinkling. "Eli. This has nothing to do with Joe. It has everything to do about you and me. And what marriage means. I marry you," she said, "and it's forever. Until death parts us. I want to be absolutely sure."

"So you're not saying no. You're just saying you need more time."

She nodded. "A little more time. That's all."

Eli let out a sigh of relief. He would have preferred she'd just said yes, but at least she wasn't saying no. "Can I ask how soon you'll be ready? A day from now? A year?"

She smiled. "Maybe somewhere in-between?" she teased.

"All right. Fine. I should gather my children." He turned away from her to go and then came back again. "You know I'm going to keep asking until you say yes."

"I hope so," she said.

And then she smiled at him in a way that warmed him from the tip of his toes to the top of his head, and Eli walked around the display of poinsettias to join the crowd, thinking he might be the most blessed man on Earth.

Chapter Eleven

Eli stood in the rear of the schoolroom, watching his neighbors and friends, both Amish and English, as they moved from desk to desk, sampling cookies and making purchases. Ginger's stepbrother Ethan and his wife, Abigail, had done an excellent job of organizing the Christmas cookie sale. Abigail had enlisted the help of the women, young and old, in Hickory Grove to make dozens of cookies, hundreds of dozens, to sell as a fundraiser for the school. Mothers made cookies with their daughters, grandmothers made cookies with granddaughters and adult sisters like Tara, Nettie, Ginger and Lovey made cookies together. One of Benjamin's Englisher customers, a retired schoolteacher, had even baked cookies to donate when she heard about the cause.

With more Amish families moving to Kent County each year, the schoolhouse was bursting at the seams. The original idea had been to build an addition to the structure to accommodate the extra students, but at an elders' meeting that week, it had been decided that a new school needed to be built on the other end of town, if they could raise enough money. One of the new families around the corner from Eli had even offered to donate an acre of ground. With a couple of fundraisers as successful as this one and the help of all of the tradesmen in Hickory Grove, Eli had the feeling they'd have a new schoolhouse in no time.

He nibbled on a cookie Ginger had given him as she'd passed by carrying a wooden crate of cookies from their family buggy. It was as good a piece of gingerbread as he'd ever eaten. She'd made them herself, she'd told him. His gaze moved about the room until it settled on her. Tonight she was wearing a green dress the color of summer grass that made her eyes all the greener. She wore a white prayer kapp to cover her blond hair, the string of the *kapp* a loop that brushed the nape of her neck, where tendrils of her hair curled. His hand itched to touch those little wisps, but he would never do that. He didn't think the age difference between him and Ginger mattered that much, except in the circumstances of physical intimacy. While he knew very well that young folks engaged in kissing and such while courting, at his age, and as a widower and a father, he didn't feel it would be appropriate. Ginger's parents or even someone in the community might look at such behavior as him taking advantage of the younger woman, and he would never want that. He was so set on proper behavior that he had decided he wouldn't kiss Ginger, though he wanted to, until they were properly wed before God, their bishop, friends and family.

He watched Ginger. She was standing behind her younger sister Nettie, showing her how to use a spatula to ease cookies onto a scale. The women were selling the cookies by the pound so folks could buy as many varieties as they wished. Most of the buying customers were Englishers, and they didn't even seem to blink at what Eli had feared would be too much per pound for anyone to buy cookies at all.

"*How much* a pound?" Eli had overheard an Englisher woman with her elderly mother in tow ask earlier in the evening.

Ginger's fraternal twin sister, Bay, had repeated the price, and the woman, wearing a bright red hat with a white pom-pom on top, had chuckled with glee. "Home-made cookies? We'd pay twice for that, wouldn't we, Mom?" she'd said. "I'd pay anything, so I don't have to make them."

"Twice that," her mother had agreed, pulling a fat wallet from her handbag. "No one bakes anymore."

The mother and daughter had made Eli smile as they'd moved from desk to desk, checking out the cookies and even sampling some. Bay, who had as good a head for business as anyone Eli had ever known, had come up with the clever idea of passing out samples of some of the cookies, ones that had gotten broken being transported. Eli had a feeling that trick would guarantee they would sell every cookie that had been carried into the schoolhouse that evening.

"Pretty impressive turnout," Ginger's stepfather said, walking over to stand beside Eli. Benjamin had a bit of a limp these days. A flare-up of gout, he'd told Eli earlier in the week. Eli liked Benjamin immensely. He admired him as a man of faith and the head of the family. He also admired how well Benjamin had handled the death of his first wife and his willingness to accept the gift of Rosemary and her son and daughters when God set him on their path. Rosemary's husband had been Benjamin's best friend back in upstate New York. That might have deterred a lesser man, but Benjamin was a devoted man of God, a man who had the good sense not only to pray but to listen to the answers to his prayers.

"Our wives and daughters and sisters," Benjamin went on. "They outdid themselves, didn't they?"

Eli's sister, Claudia, hadn't come to the cookie sale to volunteer because one of her girls was down with croup. However, she'd sent her oldest son over to Eli's with twelve dozen cookies for the sale and an extra dozen for Eli. She'd made one of his favorites, the candied fruit cookies that their mother had made for them as children. With assorted nuts and dried fruits like pineapple, dates and cherries, the cookies always reminded him of fruitcake. Claudia now continued their mother's tradition each year, making multiple batches for her family and Eli's.

Benjamin and Eli stood side by side, watching the ladies sell box after box of cookies. They had set up an assembly line on the school desks. The teenage girls placed cookies into boxes that the customers picked up when they came in the door. Then the older women weighed the cookies, taking money and making change from an old fishing-tackle box someone had brought to serve as a cash box. Little girls were helping at each of the stations. Lizzy was standing with Tara and talking nonstop.

Ginger had indeed brought his shy daughter out of her shell. To see his Lizzy so comfortable with Tara, someone she would have once considered a stranger, even though she knew Benjamin's family, made Eli's heart sing. After his Elizabeth had died, one of his greatest fears had been that he wouldn't be able to raise their children to be the men and woman his wife wanted them to be. Since Ginger had come into his life, that fear was gone. The blended Miller-Stutzman family had embraced his in an even tighter hug since Eli and Ginger had begun walking out together, and he saw in his mind's eye the families only getting closer with the years.

Eli's gaze naturally wandered to Ginger again. The line of customers was no longer out the door, which was a good thing because when she'd last walked past him, she'd told him she was bringing in the last of the cookies they had to sell.

"Rosemary said you and the children will be coming to our place Christmas Eve for supper and prayer," Benjamin said. "I was glad to hear it. We like to keep Christmas quietly, but it's always nice to have another family join us."

"It was kind of you to ask us. We usually join Claudia's family, but she's got her in-laws coming in from Tennessee, and the house and kitchen will be bursting. And truth be told, her mother-in-law can talk until a man's ears ache, so…" Eli's voice drifted off as Benjamin chuckled.

Several of the unmarried men of the community came into the schoolhouse in a burst of bitter cold and rowdy male voices and began moving desks back to their proper places as the women sold the last of the cookies.

"Seen a big change in Ginger these last months," Benjamin mused aloud. "Since you hired her to look after your little ones. She's set aside her girlish ways and become a young woman right in front of us."

"Ginger's truly been an answer to my prayers," Eli responded. "Here I was, worried whether or not I could even take the job Ader had offered, especially with Lizzy being so sick at the time, and Rosemary walks up to me in Byler's. The next thing I know, Ginger's coming to work for me."

"'For my thoughts are not your thoughts, neither are your ways my ways, saith the Lord. For as the heavens are higher than the earth, so are my ways higher than your ways, and my thoughts than your thoughts,'" Benjamin quoted from the book of Isaiah.

"*Ya*," Eli agreed. He wasn't much for being able to recite scripture, but he was good at remembering their meaning when it was quoted to him. He knew this one because it was something his grandfather used to say. "The Lord works in mysterious ways."

"That he does," Benjamin agreed. Then he met Eli's gaze, taking on a serious tone. "I know I'm not supposed to get involved with our adult children's lives. Rosemary tells me that all the time. We have to accept that we've raised them right, and they'll make good decisions, but I have to ask, Eli. What's your intention with our Ginger?"

Benjamin's directness took Eli by surprise. But he wasn't insulted or embarrassed, he just hadn't anticipated the question tonight. "My *intention*?" he asked. He didn't have to think on it because it was all he'd been thinking about for weeks. "My intention is the same as any man's when he walks out with a woman. At least a man my age, with a houseful of children." He paused, unprepared for the emotion that welled in his chest. "I intend to ask Ginger to marry me. When the time's right. Now I know there's an age difference, Benjamin, but—"

"That's no concern of ours, mine and Rosemary's," Benjamin interrupted. "Had it been, we'd have said so from the start."

"My sister might not agree."

Benjamin gave a wry smile, and for a moment, they both watched an English couple arguing over what kind of chocolate chip cookies they wanted.

"Claudia's expressed the same concern to Rosemary," Benjamin said.

Eli looked at him, feeling a speck of irritation. He was a grown man. He didn't need his sister in his business. "She has?" He frowned. "Claudia should mind her own knitting."

Benjamin waved his meaty hand in dismissal. "Women's talk. Claudia meant no harm. You're her little brother. It's natural she be protective of you and your little ones."

"I know," Eli agreed. "I just worry that no one will suit her unless she chooses for me, and that's not going to happen. You know she and Elizabeth were good friends. Closer to sisters."

Benjamin nodded in commiseration. "I hear what you're saying." He cut his eyes at Eli. "I'd ask that you not tell Claudia I tattled, else I'll be in trouble with my wife."

"No fear of that." Eli exhaled. "Anyway, like I was

saying. I want to marry Ginger. I think she and I are well matched. We find it easy to go about the tasks of the day together. We think along the same lines. We work well together and talking is easy." He smiled. "Ginger's so full of life that she brought life back into our home. Into me."

"I agree you're well matched. More importantly, Rosemary agrees." Benjamin tucked his thumbs beneath his suspenders and tugged at them. "So what are you waiting for?"

Eli looked at Benjamin, not sure what he meant. "What?"

"You've known Ginger since we moved to Hickory Grove, and she's been in your household for months. I think maybe it's time you ask her to marry you," Benjamin said.

"I, um… We—Ginger and I—agreed to wait awhile before we made that decision. To…take our time."

"But you *want* to ask her to marry you?" Benjamin looked Eli directly in the eye.

"*Ya, ya,*" Eli stumbled, suddenly feeling uncomfortable. "I do."

"Then I say you best ask and make it official. I don't believe in long courting or betrothal for that matter. And in this case, if it's what you both want, I think it's best you get to it. Especially with *him* prowling about." Benjamin lifted his chin in the direction of the far side of the room.

Eli saw at once who his friend was pointing out. Joe Verkler, who must have come in with the young men to clean up, was standing next to Ginger as she cleaned cookie crumbs from a school desk. They were having a private conversation and she was laughing.

The way a girl laughs with her beau.

Eli felt his heart tumble. Joe was such a handsome young man and Ginger was so gorgeous. Too pretty a girl for Eli, with his wrinkles and his gray hair. They were a good-looking couple, too. And Ginger seemed to be happy, the way she smiled up at him. Eli couldn't hear her laughter over the voices in the room, but he could hear it in his head. Had she ever looked that way when she talked to him?

Eli slid his hands into his pants pockets and swallowed hard. Suddenly he felt overheated. A voice in the back of his head made him wonder if Claudia had been right from the beginning. *Was* Ginger playing him? Had she agreed to court Eli because she wanted to make Joe jealous? Was Joe who she still wanted to marry, not him? Was that why she'd put him off last week?

Eli wondered if he *was* too old for Ginger. He'd been telling Claudia and himself that he wasn't. He'd even been trying to prove it to Ginger, but what if he was wrong? What if this had all been a mistake, these weeks of courting the prettiest girl in the county? Was he just being selfish?

Maybe Ginger deserved a younger man. One without children already, too. Ordinarily, a young woman had time to adjust to married life, then the duties of a mother came on slowly as the children came one by one. If Eli married Ginger, she would walk away from the wedding ceremony the mother of four with the responsibilities of a big farm and five to wash and cook and clean for.

Eli's mouth became dry and he could feel his heartbeat increase. Was he so lonely that his judgment had been off? Was he not really suited to be Ginger's husband?

Eli felt sick to his stomach. If it *was* a mistake, he might be ruining not only Ginger's life but that of his children.

Benjamin clamped his hand over Eli's arm. "No time like the present time, eh?"

Suddenly resigned, Eli watched as Benjamin walked away. His friend was right. If he was going to do this, there was no need to put it off.

Eli gathered his children one by one and put them into the buggy. As he did so, he kept an eye out for Ginger, glancing over his shoulder again and again. The schoolyard was lit with kerosene lanterns and the lamps from departing buggies.

He'd caught Ginger without Joe at her side and asked her if she had a minute to talk. She was just packing up the scale and the last few bakery boxes they hadn't used. He'd told her he'd get his four little ones situated in the buggy and then be back into the school to see if anything needed to be carried out.

"Can we have a cookie, *Dat*?" Lizzy asked. She was on the front seat, bundled in a thick denim coat, a wool hat and wool mittens. Her brothers had piled into the back and were wrestling like puppies on the floor. The buggy rocked.

"*Sohns*! In your seats," Eli ordered, tucking a blanket over Lizzy's legs.

"Cookies!" Phillip shouted. "We need cookies. Did you buy us cookies, *Dat*?"

"No one *needs* cookies," Eli responded, trying not to be short with him. He wiped a cookie crumb off Lizzy's cheek, easily seen with the bright lights he'd recently installed in the buggy.

The interior lights ran off a car battery. He'd added a little heater, as well. In his day, his mother had heated bricks on the stove, wrapped them in kitchen towels, and that was what had warmed them on cold trips in the buggy. But Eli didn't have the time or energy for heating bricks on the stove, plus he worried about the danger of the children being burned by them if they were too hot.

"One cookie each," Eli conceded, opening one of the white bakery boxes at Lizzy's feet. He'd bought two boxes of cookies. Four and a half pounds in all. He gave Lizzy her cookie first. "Anyone else wanting a cookie needs to sit down," he warned his boys.

One by one, they found a place on the bench seats that faced each other, and one by one, he gave them sugar cookies. Made by one of the older Fisher girls, they were Christmas trees that were frosted with green icing and had little bits of brown icing on them that looked like pine cones.

"I have to run inside. Stay put. All of you," Eli warned, raising his finger and speaking in his best fatherly tone. "Simon, you're in charge. That means everyone has to listen to Simon until I get back. I won't be long." Eli closed the buggy door and strode across the frosty grass toward the schoolhouse.

Ginger was suddenly a bundle of nerves. Eli had come to her a few minutes ago and asked if he could talk to her. *Privately.* She knew at once what he wanted to talk about. And to her surprise, she realized she was ready to talk about it, too. About making their courtship official. About moving on to the betrothal stage. She knew she'd been the one to tell him she wanted to take things slowly, and she had at first, but in the last couple of days, she'd realized she wanted to finalize the matter and to be able to call Eli her own publicly. Because, as she had suspected, she was in love with him. Had been for weeks, maybe since she started working for him. It had just taken her a little while to see it. To accept it. Maybe because it was nothing like what she had dreamed it would be.

In girlish expectation, Ginger had thought love would hit her hard, maybe even feel like she was falling. Like the time she'd tumbled from the hayloft when she was a girl and had felt all dizzy and light as she'd tumbled. Because that was what people said, you *fall* in love. Her love for Eli had come on slowly and quietly; it had been like a warmth that she had first just felt in her fingertips as they brushed his when she took her turn at Chinese checkers or handed him a plate for the supper table. As the days had passed, the warmth had spread in her until now she flushed from her toes to her cheeks every time she laid eyes on him. She wanted to be with Eli every minute of the day, and when they were apart, she missed him terribly. She missed his calm, steady voice, his kindness, his practicality, but mostly she missed the way he talked to her, the way he treated her. He had spoken of love, but more importantly, she saw it in his eyes every time he looked at her.

Eli had told Ginger he'd be back in to see if anything else had to be carried out of the school. But the room was already put back together just the way Ethan liked it with desks grouped rather than in rows. Joe and some of the single men had done the cleaning up and moving. She'd talked to Joe for a few minutes during the cookie sale, and she was pleased that she felt absolutely nothing for him. When he first broke up with her, she'd avoided him because her feelings had been hurt. She'd been angry and upset with him. But now, having gotten some distance from him, and with Eli in her life, she realized Joe had done her a favor. She'd told him that and they'd both had a good laugh over it.

In the cloakroom, Ginger squinted, trying to see if she could spot Eli through the frosty window. Her sisters had already walked to their buggy. They'd come in two buggies, so her mother and Benjamin had taken one home, and she and her sisters would take the other. Bay, who was driving, had asked if they should wait on Ginger or if Eli was dropping her off. It would be easy enough for him to do. Their place was on his way home. It would give Ginger and Eli a few minutes to be together, which would be nice, even with the children. It would be their first buggy ride as a betrothed couple and, for some reason, the idea of that tickled her.

Unable to see into the dark outside with the bright lights of the schoolhouse still burning, Ginger took her cloak off one of the hooks the schoolchildren used. She was just putting on her bonnet when the cloakroom door opened, and Eli walked in.

"There you are!" she said, barely able to contain her excitement. He was going to ask her to marry him; she just knew it. And she was going to say yes. While she was busy filling cookie boxes for customers, she'd decided to be bold when he asked and suggest they not wait long to marry. The fall was the usual time for weddings, but that was tradition, not *Ordung*, and they could be married when they wanted, with the bishop's permission. As she saw it, once their minds were made up, there was no need for the children to go on any longer without a woman in the house. A mother to care for them. And truthfully, now that she knew what she wanted, what God wanted for her, she didn't want to waste any time. She wanted to be Eli's wife and it couldn't happen quickly enough.

"Bay's about to leave. She asked if I was going home with them or if you were dropping me off." She smiled up at Eli. His blue eyes could change with his mood. Tonight they seemed grayish, and she couldn't recall ever seeing them that color. "Do you want to drop me off so we can have a few minutes together?"

Eli looked down at his boots. He seemed nervous. And upset. "Not sure you're going to want a ride home from me when I say what I have to say."

She frowned. What was he talking about? Did he think she was going to put him off again? Now she felt bad. And foolish. "Why wouldn't I want to ride home with you, Eli?" She took a step toward him. There were a couple of people still in the schoolhouse, including Ethan and Abigail and her son. But they were busy sweeping and collecting the lamps and lanterns they'd borrowed to light up the schoolhouse in the dark. No one was paying Ginger and Eli in the cloakroom any mind.

Eli slowly lifted his head.

Something was wrong. What, she didn't know. She waited.

"Ginger, I've been thinking, and…" He went silent.

Ginger heard the voices coming from inside the schoolroom, but she didn't hear what they were saying. The cloakroom with its fresh coat of paint seemed to shrink around them, the voices fading. Suddenly there was no one but her and Eli. And the dread she suddenly felt in the pit of her stomach.

"I think we should end this," Eli said flatly.

For a moment she didn't know what he was talking about. But then he lifted his gaze to meet hers and she knew.

She knew.

"I'm sorry," he said.

Tears sprang in Ginger's eyes. He didn't want to marry her.

"You and I, we shouldn't be…" He exhaled. "The courtship is over. I release you from any…the obligation you feel—"

"Any *obligation*?" she blurted, surprising herself. "What are you talking about, Eli?" She never lost her temper, but she lost it now. "You're breaking up with me?" she demanded. How was this possible? Eli had told her he loved her. He had— She took a shuddering breath, her heart fluttering in her chest, a lump rising in her throat.

Eli was still talking, but she barely heard him.

"Didn't mean to… Mistaken… Unfair to you to… The two of you… Better off…"

Ginger felt like she was shattering inside. Because she loved him. She loved Eli, but he didn't love her. That was what he was saying, what he obviously meant by the words she was only catching bits of.

She wanted to marry him and he didn't want to marry her. That was what it all came down to.

Ginger suddenly felt like she couldn't breathe, and she had to get outside. She had to get out into the cold and catch her breath. Get away from Eli and his betrayal. He had told her he loved her. But he hadn't meant it. He couldn't have meant it, otherwise, he wouldn't be saying these things now.

"I have to go," she managed, sidestepping to get around him.

"Ginger—"

"Bay will leave without me and…" She reached the door that led outside and she yanked it open. A cold wall of air hit her in the face.

Outside, she heard buggies making their way down the lane and out onto the paved road. Bay would leave without her, and she'd have to walk home in the cold.

"Ginger," Eli called after her as she stumbled down the steps. "You're upset. I haven't done a very good job of explaining myself." Following her, he touched her shoulder. "Ginger, please, let me explain. I don't want you to be upset with me. You'll see this is really for the best. You only have to—"

"Don't touch me, Eli, and don't speak to me," she said, her feet finding the frosty grass. She spotted their buggy. Bay had just backed up and was ready to pull into the lane.

"Ginger, wait!"

But Ginger didn't wait for him. She ran across the lane,

cutting in front of the buggy, forcing Bay to pull up hard on the reins. She threw open the door and climbed up.

"Ginger, what—"

"Please don't say anything, Bay," Ginger said softly as she slid the door shut. Nettie had vacated the front passenger seat for her and she dropped down into it. "Just drive," she said, burying her face in her hands.

Ginger stood in the doorway of the Troyers' living room watching her sister Nettie flirt shyly with a boy visiting the Troyers from Michigan. The Troyers, who owned the other harness shop in Hickory Grove, had kindly offered to give the Fishers a break and host a holiday singing. With so many folks visiting from out of town, it was the perfect opportunity for the young, single men and women of the community to meet other singles.

There had been singing, and refreshments, of course. Lettice had served mini egg salad and tuna sandwiches, coconut cupcakes that looked like they were frosted with snow and gallons of hot spiced apple cider. They sang fast hymns and then they played Change Seats. Then, when everyone was out of breath, they played some word games.

Ordinarily Ginger would have enjoyed the fun and games. But tonight, everything seemed silly and superfluous. She should never have come. She'd only done it to give the impression that she was fine with Eli breaking up with her.

Which she was not. She was brokenhearted.

Ginger was there with Joe, and he was the last person she wanted to be with. Since she'd walked in the

Troyers' door, she had wanted to go home. It had been wrong to ask Joe to bring her and her sisters tonight. She didn't want to be here with him. After walking out with Eli, she realized just how immature Joe was. She didn't want to be here at all. And she certainly didn't want to walk out with Joe again. It had been a mistake to think there was any way she could go back to the way things had been before she began keeping Eli's children. Back to the way she had been before she had fallen in love with him.

Now she just wanted to go home. But she couldn't, because Joe had brought her as well as Nettie and Tara and Bay, and they all seemed to be having a wonderful time. Even Bay, who didn't usually like social events, was enjoying herself. Ginger had seen her talking with Levi Troyer several times during the evening, and now they were standing off by themselves, conversing in private.

Ginger exhaled and looked out the farmhouse window into the dark, wondering if she could plead a headache and get Joe to run her home. Or better yet, catch a ride with someone going her way. Then she wouldn't have to speak to Joe. He could give her sisters a ride home when they were ready to go or catch a ride with someone else. She needed to get out of there before she burst into tears.

"Oh Eli," she breathed. Blinking back the moisture in her eyes, she pressed her hand to the cold glass, then rested her forehead against it. It was hard to believe that a week ago she had been so happy, and now it seemed as if she never would be again.

Chapter Twelve

Eli stood in his sister's driveway and watched as his children clambered into his buggy. The sky was gray, the air damp and cold. "Thank you for keeping them today, Claudia." He lifted Lizzy in and then closed the door against the wind and a few stray snowflakes. "I have a day or two of work left to do after Christmas to finish up the job. If you don't mind having them, I'd appreciate your help."

"Of course I don't mind." His sister followed him around to the driver's side. Her breath came in white puffs in the cold air. "They're my niece and nephews. They're always welcome here."

"I know, but with your in-laws here—" Eli wiped his mouth with the back of his gloved hand.

He hadn't seen Ginger or heard from her since he broke up with her. The Monday morning after the cookie sale, her sister Tara had shown up to watch the children. When Eli had seen Benjamin's buggy coming up the driveway, his heart had sung, thinking it was Ginger. Even considering that maybe she'd come to protest his decision, to tell him that she didn't care how old she was, that she loved him and not Joe.

But it hadn't been her.

And while it had been kind of Tara to come in her sister's stead, it had been too hard to have her in the house. Too hard when all he wanted was Ginger. So he'd asked his sister to watch his children for the two weeks it would take him to finish the job he'd taken. She'd been happy to do it and not said a single unkind word when he'd explained why Ginger wouldn't be coming to the house anymore. She'd been sweet and gentle and not pried for once, though it was apparent she knew what had happened. Everyone in Hickory Grove knew. The Amish telegraph.

To his amazement, dealing with Claudia had been much easier than with his children. Lizzy cried every night for Ginger, Phillip was misbehaving at every turn and Simon was so angry with his father that Eli didn't know what to do with him. And Andrew's response to the breakup was the most heartbreaking at all. He hadn't said a word when Eli told the children Ginger wouldn't be coming to the house again. Andrew didn't talk anymore. Not just to Eli but to anyone. It seemed like he'd built a little shell around himself, and Eli didn't know how to break through. Claudia suggested gently that he just needed to give Andrew time, that children were resilient and that they'd get over the change. Eli prayed she was right but feared she wasn't.

Ginger hadn't even gone to church last Sunday. He hadn't had the heart to ask her family why she wasn't there. Probably had a cold… That, or she'd gone to church with the Verklers over in Rose Valley. He'd heard she'd gone to a singing at the Troyers' with Joe Verkler. He'd been so upset when he heard, though he didn't know why. That was why he had broken up with her, so she could be with Joe… Or some other young man of her choice. A man deserving of her beauty and youth.

Eli opened the buggy door slowly, feeling as if he were slogging through mud. He had been this way since the night of the school fundraiser. No colors seemed as bright to him as they had been, no smells as good or sounds as sharp. He missed Ginger so much that his chest ached. He kept telling himself he'd done the right thing, but after two weeks without her, he was beginning to have second thoughts. Not that it mattered now. Ginger hadn't come to him, so obviously, she was over him. Over them.

If there had ever been a *them* to begin with.

Eli had *thought* she'd cared for him, but he kept telling himself over and over again that he had been mistaken. That he'd done the right thing. It was the only way he could get through the day right now. There was no way of getting through the nights. That was probably why he felt so exhausted, so defeated. A man couldn't live on two or three hours of sleep a night.

"Eli, I'm worried about you. Are you sure you don't want to come to supper tomorrow night for Christmas Eve?" Claudia rested her hand on his arm. "We're just having soup and bread, but it would be nice to have you with us."

"Thank you, but you've already got a houseful." He nodded in the direction of the barnyard, where several of her nieces and nephews on her husband's side were jumping into puddles to break the ice that had formed on them overnight and not melted on the gray day. "We're supposed to go to Benjamin and Rosemary's," Eli said, not trusting himself to speak Ginger's name aloud. Especially in front of Claudia. "Rosemary invited us weeks ago," he explained. "Wouldn't seem right not to go."

"I think they'd understand if you changed your mind," she said gently, pulling her cloak tighter around her shoulders.

Eli stepped up into the buggy. "The children are looking forward to going. To seeing—" He focused straight ahead, watching the children playing through the windshield, the backs of his eyes stinging.

Claudia was quiet for a moment. "Eli, maybe I was wrong," she said quietly.

Only half hearing her, he looked down. "What's that?"

"I hate to see you this unhappy. I… I've been doing a lot of thinking. And praying, and…maybe I was wrong about Ginger." She shuddered against the cold. "About the two of you. Maybe you're meant to be together after all."

Eli couldn't bring himself to look at her. He wasn't angry with his sister. It didn't matter what she had thought or what she had said. He was the one who had broken up with Ginger. Impulsively broken up with her without thinking it through, without talking about it with her. And now he was stuck with his decision. And now Ginger was dating Joe Verkler again—good-looking, flashy Joe. For all he knew, they'd be crying the marriage banns come next church Sunday.

"Eli." Claudia reached up and grabbed his arm, not so gently this time. "You should go talk with Ginger."

"Too late for that." He lifted the reins, his gelding stepped up and the buggy rolled forward. "See you Christmas Day, Claudia."

"It's never too late, Eli!" she called after him. "Not until one of you is married to another!"

Ginger sighed and tugged on her sewing needle, catching a loop of thread around her finger. She wasn't the best at hand sewing, but her skills were perfectly adequate. She knew full well how to hem a dress. She'd been whipstitching hems since she was seven. So why couldn't she do it today? How did she keep getting these little knots in her thread? And why were her stitches so uneven? She groaned and tugged again, this time so hard that the thread snapped.

"*Ach*!" Ginger muttered, dropping the dress to her lap as she reached for the scissors. She'd have to pull out enough stitches now to tie off the thread and then restitch the same three or four inches of hem she'd already stitched twice. "I just can't do anything right today," she muttered. Then as she lowered the scissors, she somehow managed to prick her hand with the needle. "Ouch!" she said loudly. She looked up to see her mother and her sisters Nettie and Tara staring at her. No one said a word.

Ginger narrowed her gaze at her sisters. "What?" she demanded in a not-so-pleasant tone. Then she pressed her injured hand to her mouth.

Her mother cleared her throat and looked to Tara and Nettie. "Could you girls make us some tea and maybe cut us a few slices of that banana bread? I just love the chocolate chips in it."

"I'm sorry," Ginger said to her mother and sisters. She looked away as tears filled her eyes. "I'm sorry," she repeated in a whisper.

Tara and Nettie both rose from their chairs, set their sewing down and left the sewing room without so much as a sound.

"Ginger," her mother said quietly when the girls were gone.

"I don't mean to be so cross." Ginger shook her head. She sniffed and pressed her chapped lips together. She set the needle down on the little table beside her and fumbled in her apron pocket for her handkerchief. She'd been using it a lot these days.

Her mother looked up from the sock she was knitting; it was so small that Ginger knew it had to be for one of her youngest brothers, Josiah or James. "I know you don't, *Dochtah*." Her knitting needles clicked together as her hands made the stitches from memory.

Ginger glanced around and realized, for the first time since they'd moved into the house here in Delaware, how much this sewing room resembled her mother's old sewing room back in New York.

Nearly square, with two large windows, this sewing room, like the old one, was painted a pale blue, with a blue-and-white-and-yellow rag rug in the middle of the floor. There were the two rocking chairs placed side by side where Tara and Nettie had been sitting. One wall boasted an oversize walnut cabinet rescued from a twentieth-century millinery shop, and open drawers revealed an assortment of various sizes of thread, needles, scissors and paper patterns. A small knotty pine table with turned legs stood between the windows. In the warmer months, her mother, who had the greenest thumb of anyone Ginger knew, kept fresh herbs and flowers planted in a terra-cotta planter there.

"Bay said you told her you wouldn't be walking out with Joe again," Ginger's mother said. "Would you like to talk about it?"

"About Joe?" Ginger arched her eyebrows. "There's nothing to talk about. You were right. He was a bad choice from the beginning. We're not well suited." She looked away. "I guess that makes you happy. To know you were right."

"It never makes a mother happy to see her child in pain." Her mother's knitting needles went still and silent. "I meant, did you want to talk about what happened between you and Eli."

Ginger sniffed and wiped her nose with her handkerchief. "*Ne*, I do not."

"Then don't talk to me about it, but you and Eli need to talk. The bad air needs to be cleared. It's hanging over us all, Ginger."

Ginger stared at the dress in her lap. She needed to finish the hem. She had to be in the harness shop in an hour's time to work her shift. Since she'd stopped watching the children for Eli, she'd gone back to working for Benjamin in his harness shop. She ran the cash register when he needed her, but mostly she worked in the back, sewing leather with a heavy-duty sewing machine powered by a large foot treadle. The work had been good for her; it helped ease the ache in her chest that came from missing the little ones so much. And

Eli. She missed Eli so much that she could barely think straight. The first few days after Eli broke up with her, she had mostly been angry, but now she was just sad. And lonely. Even in her mother's busy house that was always busting at the seams with people, she missed Eli.

Ginger's gaze strayed to a window, the glass white with frost. "I've nothing to say to Eli. He broke up with me."

"But you said you're not even sure why. Don't you think he owes you an explanation?"

Ginger's eyes teared up again. "It doesn't matter. He wanted to marry me and now—" Her voice caught in her throat. "And now he doesn't."

"But you're miserable, and from what I hear, Eli's more miserable than you are. If that's possible," her mother added.

Ginger didn't say anything. What was there to say? Eli didn't love her. And if he didn't love her, she didn't want to marry him. Because she loved him. It was as simple as that. She couldn't even remember what he'd said at the schoolhouse that night. She'd been so upset that she'd not heard or absorbed his explanation.

"Did you hear what I said?" her mother asked. "I said Eli's very upset. I think the two of you need to talk. You can't keep hiding from him."

"I'm not hiding."

Her mother rose, pushing her knitting down into the fabric bag that hung on her favorite chair, a recliner Benjamin had brought home for her when she was expecting the twins. "Oh you're hiding, all right. You sent your sister to watch the children. You went to church with Anne Yoder and her family last Sunday so—"

"Anne invited me," Ginger argued.

"So you wouldn't have to see Eli," her mother finished. "And I think you're behaving foolishly. If the two of you aren't right for marriage, that's one thing, but you're such good friends. You shouldn't lose a good friend, nor should he."

Ginger just sat there staring at the dress in her lap.

Her mother walked to the door. "I'm not convinced it's too late to set things right with Eli."

Ginger didn't look at her mother. "I am. He said he didn't want to court me. That's the end of it."

Her mother stopped in the doorway and exhaled. "We don't always mean the things we say, Ginger. You're old enough to know that." She hesitated. "Are you sure there isn't anything between Joe Verkler and you now?"

Ginger looked up. "*Ne.* There is not. Joe's not any more ready to marry and be the head of a family than Josiah or James. Honestly... I think I liked the *idea* of him more than I actually ever liked him." She glanced out the window again. It was a gray day and the wind was howling. The temperature was dropping fast. Benjamin had said at the breakfast table that morning that snow was in the forecast for the following day, Christmas Eve. A storm coming out of the west, he said.

"Just talk to Eli, Ginger," her mother murmured. "If nothing else than to clear the air and ease your pain and his."

"If I never talked to Eli again, it would be too soon," Ginger said, looking up defiantly at her mother.

"Well, that's going to be interesting, considering the

fact that he and the children are coming for supper to-morrow night."

"What?" Ginger got to her feet. "He's still coming? Can't...can't you...*uninvite* him?"

"On Christmas Eve?" Her mother raised her eye-brows. "Certainly not. Benjamin saw him at the feed store yesterday and he said he would see us tomorrow night."

Ginger crossed her arms over her chest stubbornly. "I don't want to talk to Eli. I'm not doing it."

Her mother walked out of the room, still in good humor. "We will see about that, *Dochtah*."

Ginger stood at the stove and threw the last of the vegetables into the soup. She liked to add them at dif-ferent stages, so they didn't all cook to mush.

"Could you turn the back burner on under the clam chowder?" Tara asked as she passed behind Ginger, carrying a stack of plates.

She was setting the two kitchen tables for the Christ-mas Eve meal. They were just having soup and sand-wiches, but there were an apple crisp and blueberry buckle baking in the oven, and there would be ice cream to go with the dessert. When Benjamin bought the house in Delaware, he'd added propane tanks to the property, which allowed them to run not just the refrigerator, washer and dryer, but a freezer in the cel-lar. Even after being there three years, their own freezer still seemed like such a luxury.

After supper, their family and Eli's would gather to-gether in the parlor for prayers and a short sermon that Benjamin, as the head of the household, would give.

When Ginger had heard that Eli was still coming with the children, she'd been half tempted to say she was sick and go to bed for the evening. But then she wouldn't get to see Andrew, Simon, Phillip and Lizzy and she missed them so much that she feared she would shatter if she didn't hug them. And as much as she hated to admit it, her mother was right. She couldn't avoid Eli forever.

That didn't mean she had to talk to him.

That was what she had told her mother that morning. Her mother hadn't been pleased. Ginger could tell by the way she'd pursed her mouth. But her mother hadn't said a word, which was a relief because Ginger didn't want to get into an argument with her, not on Christmas Eve. Not on any day, because her mother was a woman to be reckoned with when she got a bee in her bonnet.

"Don't the tables look so nice?" Tara chattered as she set the plates down one at a time. "I love how Bay arranged the greenery and pine cones on the center of the table. It's so pretty and smells so good."

"Whatever you've got cooking on the back of the stove smells good, too," Ginger said, trying to forget herself and her trials for a moment. Since she and Eli had broken up, she had felt very removed from her family. All her own fault, she realized, because she hadn't just been avoiding Eli, she'd been evading her family, too. Instead of leaning on them at a difficult time, she'd avoided them, making herself feel even more isolated than she had to. She'd been selfish, thinking of no one but herself. "What is it?" she asked Tara.

"Nothing to eat." Tara laughed as she put the last plate down at the head of the table where Benjamin always sat. "It's just to make the house smell good. Water with orange peels, cinnamon stick and clove."

Ginger breathed in the sweet, spicy aroma. "It smells so good, I bet you could sell it," she said, setting the wooden spoon down.

"Funny you would say that. Bay thought the same. We're going to try drying orange peels and see if we can make dried packets that can just be dumped in a pot of water. Bay thinks she can sell it in the Christmas shop next year."

Ginger smiled at her young sister. "I think that's a great idea."

"Ginger?" Their mother bustled into the room carrying a child-size chair in each hand. Though the little ones usually sat at the big table, with Eli's children coming, she'd decided at the last minute to set up a small table for them. She'd found a little table and chairs that had been brought from New York in the attic and she was now setting them up. "Could you do me a favor?"

Ginger took a teaspoon from a drawer. "What do you need? Both soups are on, but turned down." She dipped the spoon in the vegetable-beef soup and tasted it. It was the perfect balance of broth and meat and vegetables with just the right amount of salt.

"Could you go in the living room and set up some games? Maybe puzzles for the children, Chinese checkers and that game with the spinner?" She set the little chairs down. "Jacob put up two more tables."

"Sure." Ginger set the spoon in the sink and washed her hands. "We're playing games tonight? I thought we were just having family prayers and turning in early."

Her mother gave a wave. "You know Benjamin. He

gets ideas in his head," she said, walking out of the kitchen. "Sometimes it's just easier to go along than to argue. You best do it now," she said as she disappeared down the hall. "I think Eli is here, so we'll eat soon."

Drying her hands, Ginger took a couple of deep breaths. Just hearing Eli's name made her heart patter in her chest. But after spending a long time in prayer that morning, she had decided that she wasn't going to behave so childishly anymore. She was a grown woman whose romance hadn't worked out. And it was time she behaved like an adult.

"Keep an eye on the soups, will you, Tara?" Ginger asked as she went down the hall.

"*Ya*," Tara called after her.

In the living room, Ginger found the two small tables Jacob had brought up from the cellar. She discovered that he had also started a fire in the fireplace, which made the big living room warm and cozy. "So we're playing games," she said to herself under her breath. That meant Eli would likely stay later.

But she could handle that, she told herself as she took three boxes of puzzles down from the bookshelf and set them on the table farthest from the fireplace. Then she went back to the shelf for the Chinese checkers game. *I'll be fine. I'll do puzzles with the children. Eli and I are adults. We can certainly be in the same room together.*

But she wasn't fine. As she started setting up the Chinese checkers board, taking the brightly colored marbles from the box, a lump rose in her throat. How many hours had she and Eli spent at his kitchen table talking and laughing and playing Chinese checkers?

When she looked back now, it all seemed like a dream. A wonderful dream.

"It's in the living room," Ginger heard her mother say to someone. "Let me show you. I don't know what's wrong with it, but a three-legged table won't work, will it?"

Ginger heard someone respond, but couldn't make out what he said. The voice was male. One of her brothers, she guessed.

"It's old, but I think it still has years of use left in it." Ginger's mother walked into the living room.

Eli followed in her footsteps. He was in the living room before he saw her. Their gazes met and he froze. Ginger froze. Eli's eyes opened wide, and for a moment, he looked like one of the farm animals cornered in a barn.

Ginger's mother backed into the doorway.

Eli glanced at her. "There isn't a wobbly table in here, is there?"

"There is, but that's not why I brought you in here." Her mother rested her hands on her hips. "I brought you in here, Eli, because the two of you need to talk." She shook her head. "Honestly, I don't know which of the two of you is more stubborn. You deserve each other, I say."

"I have nothing to say to him," Ginger said, surprised by how loud and clear her voice came out, because she was trembling inside.

"Then it's going to be a long night, because no one in these families is eating until this matter is settled. One way or the other." Her mother backed out of the room, grabbing the doorknob.

"*Mam*, you're closing the door on us? What are you doing?" Ginger made for the door.

"My children…" Eli managed.

"I'm doing what I should have done two weeks ago," Ginger's mother declared. "Making you talk to each other." She looked to Eli. "Your children are fine."

"*Mam*!" Ginger protested. "You can't—I don't want to talk to him," she called after her.

"Then play a game of Chinese checkers," her mother called back.

Then the door lock clicked.

"You're locking us in?" Ginger cried, angry and horrified at the same time.

"I'll be back to check on you in a little while," she heard her mother say.

Ginger stood there for a moment staring at the locked door, hearing her mother's footsteps as she went down the hall. *She had locked them in?* Ginger couldn't believe this was happening! She turned to Eli. "I'm sorry. I didn't know anything about this."

He frowned. "Me, either."

She just stood there for a moment, looking at him. Then swallowed hard and looked away. *No tears*, she told herself. *No tears.*

After a moment, Eli cleared his throat and spoke. "Would you like to…" He exhaled. "Let's play. She'll have to let us out eventually." He gave a half-hearted chuckle. "I have to milk come morning."

Ginger pressed her lips together in indecision. She didn't want to play checkers with Eli. She didn't want to sit so close to him. She didn't want to look at him, because it would only make her sad. But she was locked in the room with him, and what other choice did she have? She could play a game with him or stand here like a scarecrow in the garden.

"Fine," she said. "I'll be green."

At the table, Ginger sat down first and moved a marble, not even waiting for Eli to take his seat. He moved and then she moved again. They each took five turns before either spoke a word. It was Eli, God bless him, who broke the impasse.

"Ginger, I want to tell you how sorry—"

"Do you realize how much you hurt me, Eli?" Ginger burst out, startling them both. "One minute we were talking about marriage and the next you're saying you're breaking up with me." She opened her arms wide. "I don't even know why."

"So you could be with a man your own age," he said as if that was obvious. "Be with Joe. Which is what I assume you wanted because you're courting again."

"Joe and I are not courting. Who told you that?"

"Eunice Gruber."

She rose from her chair and started to pace. "I'm *not* courting Joe. I went with him to a singing, thinking maybe I could give him a second chance, but I couldn't do it. Because he's not right for me and I'm not right for him. I was just so angry with you, so hurt that I… I…" She looked at him. "I think I did it for spite and—" Her voice caught in her throat. "And I'm sorry. That's not very becoming of a woman of faith. That's not who I am."

Eli rose from his chair and came to her. "If we're making confessions, I have to say, I think half the reason I told you I didn't want to court you was because I was jealous of Joe."

She drew back in disbelief. "Jealous of Joe? Whatever for? Joe Verkler isn't half the man you are, Eli. He... He's not even a man. He's a boy!"

Eli pressed his hand to his forehead. "I just... I saw the two of you together at the cookie sale and he was so handsome, and you were so beautiful and the two of you were laughing together, and I just... I thought you two deserved each other. And I didn't deserve you," he said quietly. "I think I just got scared and... I lost my way for a moment. Not very becoming of a man of faith," he finished quietly.

Ginger stood there looking at Eli for a moment and then said softly, "But Eli, I think you're the most handsome man in the world. The kindest, the—" She hesitated, thinking she shouldn't say any more, but if she didn't say it now, she would never say it. And if she was ever going to recover from this, she had to speak the truth here and now, even if it would make no difference. "I think you're the kindest, the gentlest, most family-devoted man I've ever known. You're smart and funny and you can cook and clean and..." She was fighting tears again. "And I love that you take your boots off in the house. I love you for all of those things."

Eli started to laugh and Ginger had no idea why, but suddenly she was laughing, too.

"You love me because I take my boots off, even though I have holes in my socks?"

She was still laughing, trying not to cry. "I loved you more for the hole in your sock."

"But I'm older than you. I have gray hair and children

and a dead wife and—" He stopped, his gaze meeting hers. "And you don't care about those things, do you?"

She shook her head slowly. "I don't. And I never did."

Eli stood there for a moment and then reached for her hand. When he took it, when she felt the warmth of his touch, all of the pain of the last two weeks fell away. Nothing mattered but the feel of his hand and his eyes on her.

"Ginger, I've been a fool. I asked God to find me a wife and He delivered you literally to my door. I asked and He answered my prayers and then I didn't listen. I didn't obey as I should have. I allowed myself to be undermined by self-doubt, and I am so sorry. Can you forgive me?"

She nodded, not trusting herself to speak.

"Then let me ask you another question. I have to ask. And it's fine if you say no. I'll understand if you do. Why you would." He squeezed her hand, looking down, then lifted his gaze. "Ginger, will you marry me? Will you marry this silly old fool?"

A sigh of relief escaped her lips. "*Ya*," she whispered, and then, she didn't know if he drew her into an embrace first or if she just threw her arms around him. Either way, she was in his arms.

"You will?" he asked, laughing but sounding as if he might cry at the same time.

She nodded and hugged him tight and then lifted her head from his shoulder to look into his eyes. "*Ya*, I'll marry you."

He smiled. "You know," he said softly. "I had made up my mind that I wouldn't kiss you until we were wed.

It didn't seem fitting that a man my age should kiss a young woman of—"

Ginger pressed her mouth to his and, at that moment, had there been even a sliver of doubt in her mind that she and Eli were meant for each other, it was washed away in an instant. As his lips touched hers, she knew in her heart of hearts that she was kissing her husband.

"Does this mean you've mended your differences?"

Startled by her mother's voice, Ginger backed out of Eli's arms, bringing her fingers to her lips where his kiss still burned. How had her mother gotten into the living room? Ginger hadn't even heard her unlock the door!

"I think it does," Eli managed, his face turning red.

"*Goot.* The Christmas gift I was praying for." Her mother turned to go. "Let's have supper, and later we'll talk about the wedding over a cup of hot cider."

Their gazes met and they both laughed, then Eli took Ginger's hand and led her into the kitchen to begin their new life together.

Epilogue

One year later

Ginger heard the crunch of snow beneath Eli's boots as he came up the walk from the barn. "All fed and tucked in for the night. The mare's hoof is—" She heard him start up the porch steps and stop. "Wife, what are you doing?"

She glanced over her shoulder at her husband and grasped the stepladder to keep her balance. The wind was blowing and the snow had just begun to fall. Their original plan had been to go to her mother and Benjamin's for supper and family prayers, but with the snowstorm coming in, they had decided to stay safe and warm at home. In an hour's time, Ginger had cobbled together a nice meal. There was beef stew simmering on the stove, biscuits baking in the oven, and they had a cookie jar full of treats she and the children had made that morning.

"Trying to rehang the wreath we made," she explained. The wind whipped at the wool scarf, tugging it off her head. It was the wind that was the culprit in blowing the wreath off the door in the first place. "But my fingers are so cold, I can't get the string back on the nail," she explained, showing him her hands with her fingerless gloves. She'd thought it would be easier to return the wreath to its place wearing the gloves, but she hadn't anticipated the windchill factor.

"Get off that ladder before you hurt yourself," Eli said, taking the last porch steps two at a time. When he reached her, he offered his hand. "I'll put it back up. You go inside and get warm."

Ginger accepted his hand and came down the slippery ladder, but when she reached the bottom, she didn't let go. "The children are eager to open their gifts. I think maybe you're right. I should never have left them out where they would see them."

It wasn't really an Amish tradition to give gifts for Christmas, but her mother had always given each of them a gift as children, and Eli's mother had done the same, so they had agreed there would be a gift for each child, but only one. The two younger boys had gotten wooden toys Eli had made, Lizzy had gotten a doll and Simon had gotten a brand-new shiny pocketknife. Ginger had wrapped them in bits of fabric from her sewing chest and tied them with ribbon she'd gotten from Bay at the greenhouse.

"Do you think we should open them tonight or in the morning?"

Eli drew her into his arms. "I think tonight is fine. We have the candies and oranges for them for tomorrow, and the socks and scarves you knitted."

Ginger smiled up at him and then rested her head on his shoulder for a moment. Despite the bitter cold, she was immediately warmed by his embrace. Ten months into their marriage and she still marveled at how comfortable she was as a wife, as Eli's wife. How happy she was to have him as her husband and the children as her own now.

"I've a little something for you, as well," Eli whispered in her ear.

She looked at him with a smile. "You do? I thought we agreed to no gifts. All that money we spent on the trip after our wedding."

Though for practical reasons, few folks with small children followed the tradition of taking a journey together to visit relatives before setting up housekeeping, Eli had insisted they needed some time alone together. Leaving the children with Claudia, they had gone to upstate New York to visit Ginger's relatives who were still there, staying with Benjamin's daughter Mary and her husband and children. It had been a week she would remember for the rest of her days.

"It's just a little something," Eli told her, brushing her hair from her face. When her headscarf blew off, her hair had come partially undone from its knot and she could only imagine what a fright she was. But he didn't seem to mind. He kissed the top of her head. "I don't need a gift from you, Ginger. Not ever." He gazed into her eyes, his blue eyes twinkling with joy. "You are gift enough."

Ginger pressed her lips together. Actually, she *did* have a gift for him. She had thought she might wait another week before she told him, but suddenly it felt as if the right time was now. "Now that I think about it, I do have something for you, Husband. Though you'll have to wait a bit for it."

He knitted his brow. "And what is that?"

She leaned toward him and whispered in his ear.

"What?" he exclaimed, drawing back from her, but still holding her in his arms. His face was alight with joy. "Are you sure?"

She smiled up at him. "As sure as a woman can be."

"Oh Ginger." His arms around her, he lifted her off her feet. "You know you and the four *kinder* are enough for me. More than a man deserves, but I prayed... I hoped God would bless me again. Bless us." When he set her down lightly and met her gaze, his blue eyes were teary. "Thank you. For loving me. For giving the children a mother, for—" He sniffed and laughed, unembarrassed by his emotion.

Ginger couldn't stop smiling.

"And you were on a ladder!" he burst out.

She laughed. "I'm not sick. It's the most natural thing for a woman. I—"

"In the house, wife," he interrupted. "You shouldn't be out in the cold."

She took his hand. "Only if you come in with me."

"What of the wreath?" He pointed at it, lying on the porch.

She shrugged. "Put it back up tomorrow. Come on." She led him to the door. "Let's get ourselves warm and put supper on the table."

Eli brushed his lips against hers, and Ginger closed her eyes, saying a silent prayer of thanks for that happy moment and all the happy moments of their life together yet to come.

* * * * *

Dear Reader,

I hope you enjoyed Ginger and Eli's story. I was so worried that Eli wasn't going to find a woman to love, weren't you? After all, he had been looking for years and several women had turned him down when he wanted to court them. But I like to think God was saving Ginger for him! And He was certainly saving Eli for her, wasn't He?

Looking ahead to the next story set in Hickory Grove, a stranger is coming to town. Benjamin's son, Levi, a buggy maker's apprentice, is returning home with a bride his parents have never met and they are none-too-happy with the rushed wedding. Why did they marry so quickly and will Levi's parents come to love Eve as they have their other daughters-in-law? Only time will tell!

In the meantime, I wish you peace, happiness and health.

Emma Miller

Get 4 FREE REWARDS!

We'll send you 2 FREE Books plus 2 FREE Mystery Gifts.

Love Inspired books feature uplifting stories where faith helps guide you through life's challenges and discover the promise of a new beginning.

FREE
Value Over
$20

YES! Please send me 2 FREE Love Inspired Romance novels and my 2 FREE mystery gifts (gifts are worth about $10 retail). After receiving them, if I don't wish to receive any more books, I can return the shipping statement marked "cancel." If I don't cancel, I will receive 6 brand-new novels every month and be billed just $5.24 each for the regular-print edition or $5.99 each for the larger-print edition in the U.S., or $5.74 each for the regular-print edition or $6.24 each for the larger-print edition in Canada. That's a savings of at least 13% off the cover price. It's quite a bargain! Shipping and handling is just 50¢ per book in the U.S. and $1.25 per book in Canada.* I understand that accepting the 2 free books and gifts places me under no obligation to buy anything. I can always return a shipment and cancel at any time. The free books and gifts are mine to keep no matter what I decide.

Choose one: ☐ **Love Inspired Romance**
Regular-Print
(105/305 IDN GNWC)

☐ **Love Inspired Romance**
Larger-Print
(122/322 IDN GNWC)

Name (please print)

Address   Apt. #

City   State/Province   Zip/Postal Code

Email: Please check this box ☐ if you would like to receive newsletters and promotional emails from Harlequin Enterprises ULC and its affiliates. You can unsubscribe anytime.

Mail to the Reader Service:
IN U.S.A.: P.O. Box 1341, Buffalo, NY 14240-8531
IN CANADA: P.O. Box 603, Fort Erie, Ontario L2A 5X3

Want to try 2 free books from another series? Call 1-800-873-8635 or visit www.ReaderService.com.

*Terms and prices subject to change without notice. Prices do not include sales taxes, which will be charged (if applicable) based on your state or country of residence. Canadian residents will be charged applicable taxes. Offer not valid in Quebec. This offer is limited to one order per household. Books received may not be as shown. Not valid for current subscribers to Love Inspired Romance books. All orders subject to approval. Credit or debit balances in a customer's account(s) may be offset by any other outstanding balance owed by or to the customer. Please allow 4 to 6 weeks for delivery. Offer available while quantities last.

Your Privacy—Your information is being collected by Harlequin Enterprises ULC, operating as Reader Service. For a complete summary of the information we collect, how we use this information and to whom it is disclosed, please visit our privacy notice located at corporate.harlequin.com/privacy-notice. From time to time we may also exchange your personal information with reputable third parties. If you wish to opt out of this sharing of your personal information, please visit readerservice.com/consumerschoice or call 1-800-873-8635. **Notice to California Residents**—Under California law, you have specific rights to control and access your data. For more information on these rights and how to exercise them, visit corporate.harlequin.com/california-privacy.

LI20R2

SPECIAL EXCERPT FROM

LOVE INSPIRED
INSPIRATIONAL ROMANCE

*When a city slicker wants the same piece of land
as a small-town girl, will sparks fly between them?*

Read on for a sneak preview of
Opening Her Heart
by Deb Kastner.

What on earth?

Suddenly, a shiny red Mustang came around the curve of the driveway at a speed far too fast for the dirt road, and when the vehicle slammed to a stop, it nearly hit the side of Avery's SUV.

Who drove that way, especially on unpaved mountain roads?

The man unfolded himself from the driver's seat and stood to his full over-six-foot height, let out a whoop of pure pleasure and waved his black cowboy hat in the air before combing his fingers through his thick dark hair and settling the hat on his head.

Avery had never seen him before in her life.

It wasn't so much that they didn't have strangers occasionally visiting Whispering Pines. Avery's own family brought in customers from all over Colorado who wanted the full Christmas tree–cutting experience.

So, yes, there were often strangers in town.

But this man?

He was as out of place as a blue spruce in an orange grove. And he was on land she intended to purchase—before anyone else was supposed to know about it.

Yes, he sported a cowboy hat and boots similar to those that the men around the Pines wore, but his whole getup probably cost more than Avery made in a year, and his new boots gleamed from a fresh polish.

Avery fought to withhold a grin, thinking about how quickly those shiny boots would lose their luster with all the dirt he'd raised with his foolish driving.

Served him right.

Just what was this stranger doing *here*?

"And didn't you say the cabin wasn't listed yet?" Avery said quietly. "What does this guy think he's doing here?"

"I have no idea how—" Lisa whispered back.

"Good afternoon, ladies," said the man as he tipped his hat, accompanied by a sparkle in his deep blue eyes and a grin Avery could only categorize as charismatic. He could easily have starred in a toothpaste commercial.

She had a bad feeling about this.

As the man approached, the puppy at Avery's heels started barking and straining against his lead—something he'd been in training not to do. Was he trying to protect her, to tell her this man was bad news?

Don't miss
Opening Her Heart *by Deb Kastner,*
available January 2021 wherever
Love Inspired books and ebooks are sold.

LoveInspired.com